The Night the Music Died

Gregory Payette

8 Flags Publishing, Inc.

Sign up for the newsletter on my website:

GregoryPayette.com

Once or twice a month I'll send you updates and news. Plus, you'll be the first to hear about new releases with special prices. If you'd like to receive the Henry Walsh prequel (for free) use the sign-up form here: **GregoryPayette.com/crossroad**

Chapter 1

BONNIE CHAPMAN WAS FOUND face-down in the small pond at the St. Johns Town Center. A man in charge of maintenance at the center saw her lifeless body when he first got into work, before the sun came up.

Those were the only details I had, but would hear more when Bonnie's husband, James, walked out of my bathroom. "I was surprised when I heard you were a private investigator," he said as he sat down on the couch across from me.

I waited for him to get comfortable. "I guess I'm still not clear," I said. "Why wouldn't you wait for the sheriff's office to complete their investigation?"

James turned and looked through the sliding glass doors toward my balcony. "I've just heard some things about the pace they work at over there."

"There are plenty of good cops with the sheriff's office," I said.

"After the way your career turned out, I would think you'd be less generous with your assessment of the men in blue."

He continued his stare out toward the balcony and the ocean just beyond it. I gave myself a moment to gather my thoughts. "Just because my career took a turn doesn't mean I'd hold it against other law enforcement officials."

I'd known James Chapman since we were in middle school together. We both grew up in Fernandina Beach, but I'd be lying if I said his name had entered my mind since we were kids. At least not until I started seeing his mug plastered up on billboards all across the city.

James stood from the couch. "You still haven't answered me. Will you take the case?"

It was the third time he'd asked.

He said, "I have this guilt that I should have, well... I need to do something to find out what happened. I can't just sit around and wait for the sheriff's office." He walked toward the sliding glass door and looked out toward the beach. "That's a nice view." He turned to me. "You own this place?"

I shook my head as I stood from my chair. "No, it's a rental."

His eyebrows went high on his head. "Mind if I ask what you pay? I rented some of these out a few years ago. I imagine they've gone up quite a bit... especially with that view."

I didn't answer him. "James, I'm still not sure you need to hire a private investigator. Not if you're doing it just to get over some guilt... to make yourself feel better."

He turned and looked at me. "Would it make a difference if I told you I think Bonnie might've been having an affair?"

I reached for my cup of coffee—it was cold—and looked at James over the rim. I waited for him to continue.

"The truth is," he said, "I don't need that to get out."

I stepped past him and pulled open the sliding glass door, walked out onto the balcony and leaned against the railing. I turned and folded my arms, my back to the ocean. "Does that mean the sheriff's office doesn't know you think Bonnie had an affair?"

He shook his head as he stepped outside. "No, they don't."

"Why? Because you're afraid they'll suspect you if you tell them she might've been cheating on you?"

James stepped toward me and leaned with his hands on the railing. He looked out toward the ocean, but stood a little too close to me.

I took a seat in one of the Adirondacks.

With his back to me, he said, "I don't think they'd suspect me. I just didn't think they needed to know, that's all."

"It makes no sense to keep that a secret. Especially if finding the truth is what's important?"

He turned with his back to the beach and folded his arms. "I don't need that kind of press." He looked inside the apartment, likely making a judgment of my living quarters. "So you use this place as your office?"

I looked straight out toward the ocean no more than a hundred yards from my balcony. I shrugged. "I don't do much work here. Normally I meet clients somewhere else."

James nodded. "If you ever need a bigger place, you be sure to let me know."

I found it odd James's focus wasn't as much on Bonnie's death as it was on finding his next real estate client.

I said, "If Bonnie was having an affair, you're taking a pretty big risk keeping that from the sheriff's office... whether you hire me or not."

"You don't understand, Henry. I have a reputation. I mean... I portrayed this image of me and Bonnie... the love of my life. I'm sure you've seen the billboards."

I nodded.

He said, "I'm afraid if word gets out she was having an affair..." He paused. "I just can't afford to have my reputation tarnished."

I looked through the railing, toward the ocean as I hesitated to open my mouth. "But your wife is dead, James. You're obviously not going to keep that a secret. And at this point, to me, finding the truth should be more important than what people think of you."

James looked me right in the eye. "I guess that's what makes you and me somewhat different."

He was right. But I wouldn't have used the word *somewhat*.

"Okay, well... are you going to let me hire you? Maybe if you didn't make your prospective clients beg to hire you,

you wouldn't have to live in a one-bedroom apartment." He walked past me and through the open door.

I got up and followed him inside as he took a seat on the couch.

I walked past him into the adjoining kitchen and reached into the refrigerator. "You want a drink?"

He shook his head, stood from the couch and pulled a checkbook from his back pocket. "I'll give you a deposit," he said as he sat back down on the couch and leaned over his checkbook on the coffee table. He had a pen in his hand and wrote on the check, ripped it from his checkbook and walked toward me with his hand extended. "Here, take this."

I took it from him but didn't look at the amount.

"I left it blank," he said. "You never told me your fee. But it doesn't matter. I'll pay whatever you need. I signed and dated it, so just make it out to yourself or your business, whatever it's called."

I said, "Walsh Investigations." I took a quick look at the blank check. I knew I needed the money. I always did. But I hated being involved in a case when the sheriff's office had hardly gotten started. On the other hand, I knew it could take them months, as it often did. "Do you have an idea who Bonnie was having an affair with?"

James shook his head. "I don't. But I'd put a pretty good bet on it. The cops don't even know who else she was with that night. Honestly, I'm not even sure who she'd been hanging around with lately."

I put the check under a magnet on the refrigerator and stared at it for a moment.

"Henry, I'll pay you whatever you want. Double your fee if you have to. From what I hear, you're one of the best."

I reached out and shook his hand. "I need more information. If we get together again soon—maybe later today—we can get started."

James pulled out his phone and looked at the screen. "I have a closing at three o'clock. Then I'm meeting with prospective sellers..." He turned and looked through the open glass doors toward the beach, then back down at his phone. "Then I'll need to swing by the office." He put his phone back in his pocket. "Can you come by my house around eight?"

I pulled a card from my pocket and handed it to him. "Just do me a favor. Call me if anything changes. Otherwise, I'll see you tonight."

Chapter 2

I DROVE OUT TO visit Charlie Senecal, one of my oldest friends and Chief of the Fernandina Police Department. I'd hoped he could provide some insight into James and Bonnie Chapman, who at one time had lived in Fernandina Beach. I knew if anybody knew something about their early history together, it would be Charlie.

Peggy Jenkins sat at the front desk with her eyes on her computer and looked up when she saw me walk through the door. She jumped from her chair, ran around her desk and wrapped her arms around me as she planted a wet kiss on my cheek. "*Henry Walsh!*" she said as she eased up on her grasp. "What a pleasure it is for me when you step through those doors." She walked back around to her desk and sat down in her chair with her arms folded. She stared up at me with a smile on her face. "You sure do look good."

I felt my face fill with warmth. "It's nice to see you, Peggy," I said. "You look pretty good yourself."

Peggy had aged a bit, of course, but still had that beauty she had back in high school when every boy had a crush on her. She was older than me; old enough to babysit me through the years. In fact at the time I was probably a little old to have a babysitter, but I didn't mind.

She shrugged. "I think I'm doing all right." She moved papers around her desk. It was the same desk she'd had since she graduated high school and took the job with the police. She'd worked for three different chiefs over the years and probably knew as much about what'd gone on around town as anybody. That included the other four officers who worked under Charlie.

"So what brings you back up here?" she said. "I heard what happened to your boat... hard to believe." She pushed her chair back and crossed her legs. "Where are you living now?"

"I rent an apartment right on Neptune Beach."

She nodded with approval. "That sounds nice. At least you're a little closer to home."

But home for me was no longer Fernandina Beach, assuming that's what she meant.

She smiled. "Well, I know you didn't come here to see me..." She turned and looked down the hall toward Charlie's office. His door was closed. "He just took a call. The mayor's son got into some trouble last night. One of the officers took him in. Drunk and disorderly. I'm sure the mayor would like to get it taken care of before word gets out. But you know how Charlie is about those situations."

I looked around the office. Not much had changed.

Peggy took a sip from her glass. "Can I get you a drink?"

"No, thank you."

"You sure? Charlie has some cokes back there in the fridge, if you'd like me to get you one?"

I waved my hand up in front of me. "Maybe later. I'm okay for now."

Peggy stuck a pair of glasses on her face and looked at her computer screen, both of us quiet for a bit after we'd burned through the small talk. She pulled off her glasses. "How about mom and dad? They doing okay?"

I nodded. "Yeah, they're okay." I glanced down the hall toward Charlie's office.

"Where'd you say they live, Port Charlotte?"

"Naples."

"That's nice. Judge Judy lives there."

"Oh yeah? I didn't know that."

"Mom's doing okay?"

"Good days and bad. They keep busy, though. My dad doesn't like to sit still. He said that's the key... keep moving. Don't let old age catch up to you."

Peggy laughed just as I heard the crack of a door as it opened from down the hall.

Charlie walked out of the office and down the hall toward us, but his eyes were on Peggy, shaking his head as he moved closer. "Son of a bitch must've reminded me fifteen times I'm in an appointed position. Passive aggressive little..."

Peggy looked Charlie in the eye and nodded toward me, practically standing right behind him.

Charlie turned, looked at me over his shoulder and then reached out his thick hand and wrapped it around mine, pulled me toward him and gave me a hug like a bear. He slapped me on the back and stepped back. "Jesus, lucky you weren't someone from the mayor's office." He shook his head. "The things I gotta deal with in this job." He waved me toward his office and headed down the hall. He stopped and turned to Peggy. "We're dropping all charges on the boy."

"Politics," I said. "Sucks the fun out of the job, doesn't it?"

Charlie was still shaking his head as he walked through the door to his office. He waited for me to come in and closed the door behind me.

His office looked the same as it always had. It was the same desk, the small table with the same four wooden chairs. There wasn't much else in Charlie's office other than paper piles everywhere I looked.

"I got your message," he said. "Not sure what I can do to help. As far as I know, Bonnie and James moved from here, down Southside..." He squinted his eyes. "Actually, San Marco, I believe."

"That's where they lived," I said.

"Aside from seeing his goofy face plastered on the buses and billboards all over the highways, I haven't seen him in years. I don't remember the last time." Charlie sat down behind his desk. "What a shame about what happened to Bonnie."

"Last I heard, they haven't been able to prove foul play." I sat down in one of the chairs in front of his desk.

Charlie leaned forward as he twisted a pencil between his fingers, his elbows on his desk. "You're not somehow involved in this, are you?"

I hesitated a moment, looked out the window overlooking the center of town. "James came to see me out at my apartment in Neptune Beach."

Charlie tossed the pencil on the desk and leaned back in his chair. He put his hands behind his head, his big elbows extended out on either side of him. "It's still under investigation, from what I've heard. What's he need you for?"

"To be honest, I don't have much information. Truth is, he's already asked me to keep some important details to myself."

Charlie's face got a bit twisted. "Keep the important details to yourself? What in God's name is *that* supposed to mean? You've got something he wants you to keep from the sheriff's office?" Charlie kept his stare on me.

"He said Bonnie might not've been faithful," I said.

Charlie straightened himself out and again leaned forward on the desk. "So is he hiring you to find out if she was fooling around? Or does he suspect there might've been foul play?"

"I had the same question myself. But if she was out with the person she may have been fooling around with... then maybe that'll present some information that—"

"That you'll share with the sheriff's office? I hope that's what you were about to say."

11

"He's more concerned it doesn't get out that she might've been having an affair."

"Let me guess... it'll tarnish his reputation?"

I broke a slight smile. "I guess you know James?"

Charlie shook his head. "Nah, not really. But I know his kind, more worried about the image than anything else. Am I right?"

I didn't answer, but Charlie *was* right.

He got up from his desk and walked to the window. He leaned with one shoulder against the wall as he looked down toward the street. "Why even hire you in the first place? Why not just let it lie?"

"I don't know. I'm meeting him tonight. Hopefully get a little more out of him."

Charlie turned from the window, walked toward the door and pulled it open. He stepped out into the hall and came back a moment later with two cans of Coke. He put one down in front of me, sat down at his desk and leaned back in his chair.

I said, "Any chance you can get me some information from the sheriff's office?"

Charlie popped open the top of his can. "I need to be careful. I feel like I'm on thin ice as it is. I get involved with something like this—especially out there in Jax where the sheriff's office is involved—there's no telling what it'd do to my career."

"I already have Alex doing some digging. But she's hit some dead ends. I know you have friends over there, thought maybe you could make a call?"

Charlie looked past me, toward the open door. "I can find out who's working the case, if that's what you mean." He looked at his watch. "I'll do what I can. But I also want to warn you... James Chapman's no saint, by any means. That squeaky-clean image he's trying to protect?" He shrugged. "Maybe I'm wrong, but I don't remember him to be much of a straight shooter."

Chapter 3

James Chapman's house was a long, gray stucco ranch with a tall fountain inside a circular driveway. Light sparkled off the fountain's jets as water sprayed into the air.

It was seven fifty-seven when I arrived and rang the doorbell. Musical chimes were followed by high-pitched barks from the other side of the door.

James opened the door and stood in the doorway with a small dog in his arms. Another dog hid behind him and continued to bark, its eyes right on mine.

"Don't mind him," James said. "He's all bark." He stepped back from the door and welcomed me into his house.

When he closed the door the dog he held jumped from his arms and joined the other, neither any bigger than your average-size house cat. Their barks were loud as they matched each other, bark-for-bark.

James leaned down and picked up the one he'd already had in his arms. He ran his hand down over its ears. "This one's

Bella," he said. "Give her a few minutes." He turned and looked down toward the floor. "That one's Jazz."

"Jazz?"

James nodded. "They're a bit territorial."

I extended my hand to give Bella a whiff of my scent. But she didn't seem to like what she'd smelled. She showed her teeth and snapped, missing the tip of my finger by a hair. "I guess I should give her those few minutes."

A white, life-sized statue of a naked woman surrounded by tall, green plants took up a corner of the foyer with a crystal chandelier overhead.

"Nice place," I said.

James shrugged his shoulders. "Got it for a steal during the last recession." He winked. "One man's loss is another's investment, right?" He turned and walked into the room to our left, just off the foyer.

Two couches and a single winged-back chair circled around a coffee table. Bookshelves lined the entire back wall, filled with books and framed photographs. A baby grand that took up a good part of the room under the windows. I looked out into the yard.

James let Bella down from his arms and she joined Jazz, who had already stopped barking at me... more interested in the smell of my topsiders.

"You play?" I said as I stepped toward the piano.

James shook his head. "Nothing like Bonnie, but I've tried." He stepped next to me and picked up a framed picture from the top. He handed it to me. "I don't know the last time you saw Bonnie, but I believe this is the most recent photo."

I held it in my hands and studied her face. She was as pretty as I'd remembered. She had a microphone in her hand, red, blue, and green lights surrounded her in the photo. A man who appeared to be much older than her played the drums and smiled in the background. "What kind of music did she play?"

"Everything. She had her own sound, to be honest. She mixed rock with jazz... new age. He looked down at the piano and touched a key without making a sound. "She could play anything."

"Was she performing that night?"

James shook his head. "No. She was there to watch a friend of hers perform."

My eyes went back to the picture. I felt it inside me, knowing she was no longer alive.

James took the photo from me and handed me another. "That's me and Bonnie out on a boat, with a friend of ours. That was taken a couple of years ago. Things were good back then." He turned from the piano and looked toward the other side of the room. "Would you like to have a seat?" He put the picture back and stepped toward two cabinet doors built into the wall. He turned to me. "Would you like a drink?"

A look past him into the cabinet. A bottle of Jack Daniels caught my eye. "That Jack would be all right, if you don't mind?"

He grabbed two glasses from the lowest shelf and turned to me with a different bottle in his hand. He held it out to me and said, "This is a good bourbon. Hundred-eighty-dollars a bottle. You'll like it. It's better than Jack."

I liked what I liked, and didn't fall for the trap most people did, that just because something cost more it had to've been better.

But James poured two glasses—neat—and handed one to me. He sat down on one of the couches and crossed his legs, his glass rested on his knee.

As soon as I sat down in the chair, the dogs ran back into the room. Jazz jumped up on the couch with James. Bella must've heard about the smell of my shoes, and gave them a sniff of her own before she jumped up into my lap.

"See," James said. "She likes you. Takes her a little time." He smiled, his eyes on Bella. "She must smell your dog."

I shook my head. "I don't have a dog."

James raised his eyebrows. "No? Bella normally knows a dog person right away. I'm surprised she—"

"Oh, it's not that I'm *not* a dog person. I'm just not around enough to take care of one." I ran my hand down Bella's neck and patted her on the back. "She must smell my partner's dog."

We both sat quiet for a moment.

"So why don't you tell me a little more about what happened... or what you think might've been going on with Bonnie," I said. "Maybe start with what you know about this alleged affair."

James took a sip of the bourbon, looked at the glass. "What do you think?"

"What do I *think*?"

"About the bourbon."

I took a sip. I nodded. "Not bad."

Although the truth was, I'd tried a lot of whisky and bourbon over the years. And to be honest, I drank Jack because I liked it. As far as I was concerned—no matter what kind of whiskey—after the first glass I could rarely tell the difference.

James placed his glass down on the coffee table in front of him. "As I told you, I don't know who she was fooling around with. Bonnie was very well-liked. She performed locally most of the time, at Jazz clubs around the city. Traveled around Florida once in a while, but more so when she was younger. Most of the musicians were men. The bartenders were men. So..."

"She had a lot of options? Is that what you're saying?"

James nodded and reached for his glass.

I leaned forward in the chair. "So if you don't have a particular person in mind... or a name..."

"She'd just changed so much over the past year or so. Stopped inviting me to her performances, or she wouldn't tell me where she was playing."

"But you used to go? To watch her?"

He sipped his bourbon. "When I could, I would go. But I'm busy. Especially when the real estate season kicks in."

I looked down into my glass as I'd started to acquire the taste for the expensive stuff. "Did you ever ask her about it? I mean... do you have something or someone you can point me toward? At least to give me some direction?"

Before James could answer, the doorbell rang with the same musical tones. Both dogs ran from the room with their sharp-pitched barks that made my ears ring.

James took his time and got up from his seat, his drink still in his hand. But held the glass far out from his body. Maybe to make sure he didn't spill on his pants. His walk had a swing to it as he turned the corner to answer the door.

A moment later he walked back into the room with a young woman right behind him. She had blonde hair but short as could be, without being shaved all the way down to her scalp. She was pretty, although much younger than me and James.

"Henry, this is my sister, Amanda."

I got up from the chair and gave her a nod. "Hello."

Amanda's face was red. Flushed, or maybe sunburned. She was dressed in cut-off shorts and a tank top. She had a tough look about her.

Her eyes were locked on mine for a moment. "You look familiar. Did you grow up in Fernandina Beach, too?"

I nodded. "I did."

She kept her eyes on mine for a moment longer, then turned to James. "This the private eye?"

James nodded to her, turned to me and said, "She thinks I'm being dramatic because I've hired you."

19

Amanda rolled her eyes. "I didn't say you were being dramatic. I just thought... maybe you just need to give it some time. Cops said it was an accident... she might've fallen, had too much to drink." She shrugged. "Not like it'd be the first time."

I looked at the chair behind me. Bella had jumped in and taken over my spot. I nudged her aside and sat back down with my drink still in my hand. She crawled into my lap and I looked over at James and Amanda. "Are you saying she'd fallen before from having too much to drink?"

James and Amanda looked at each other.

Amanda said, "She's been known to go overboard." She turned to James. "Remember that time she fell off the stage?"

James shook his head and rolled his eyes.

"Where'd that happen?" I said.

"River Mist Café."

"At the St. Johns Town Center?"

James narrowed his eyes, his gaze on Amanda. "I'm not sure any of this is relevant, so maybe you should just keep your comments to yourself." He stomped his way over to the couch and sat down. He threw his head back and finished the rest of his bourbon.

Amanda laughed. "You wonder why I say you're so dramatic?" She leaned against the edge of the doorway leading to the foyer and looked right at me. "I think Bonnie had been having trouble with her drinking. James doesn't want to hear it."

20

"We all need a drink to get through the day," he said, then turned to me. "Right?"

I glanced down into my empty glass and didn't answer.

James jumped up from the couch and shooed both hands toward Amanda. "Okay, I've seen enough of you for the night. Go on... on your way."

Amanda held out her open hand. "Can I have the keys?"

James scratched his head and nodded, his other hand on the side of his hip. He walked through the doorway past Amanda and disappeared without saying a word.

She kept her eyes toward the doorway, then turned back to me with a smile.

I leaned back in my seat and noticed car lights had just come on outside in the driveway. "Is someone outside waiting for you?"

Amanda nodded. "My ride. James is letting me take Bonnie's car for a little while."

"Oh." I stood and looked out the window. "It sounds like you and Bonnie didn't get along?"

She shook her head. "No, that's not the case at all. I loved her. And I miss her. She was like my big sister." She smiled and looked down toward the floor. "It was just... the last few months I felt she'd changed. She was distant... from all of us." She shrugged. "That music scene might've caught up to her."

James came back through the doorway and dangled a set of keys up in the air in front of Amanda's face. "You'd better

21

keep it all in one piece. And don't go playing around with the engine."

Amanda grabbed the keys and swung them on the ring around on her finger. She glanced back at me over her shoulder. "Nice meeting you, Henry."

James faced the foyer from the doorway. "And I don't want *you-know-who* driving her car."

The door closed, James stood with his back to me, still facing the foyer for a moment more. He turned to me, shaking his head, then walked to the window and looked out. "I don't know what she sees in that kid."

"Who's that?"

"His name's Luis." James turned, walked back toward the coffee table and picked up his empty glass. He extended his hand toward me. "You want another?"

I handed him my glass with a nod. "Her boyfriend?"

James shrugged. "I don't know what he is, exactly. She knows I don't like him." He poured me another bourbon and handed me the glass. He sipped his own drink and sat down on the couch as we both sat quiet for a moment.

"So who's this friend of Bonnie's? The one she went to see perform that night?"

James got up from the couch and pulled a framed photo down from the shelves behind the piano. He handed it to me. "Her name's Nadia."

I looked down at the photo, a picture of Bonnie with her arm around a woman equally as attractive, although younger than Bonnie.

"She's a great singer. Bonnie taught her a lot. Sort of took her under her wing. You ever want to see her, she performs at the River Mist Café a few nights a week."

I glanced at the picture again and handed it back to James. "Looks like they were pretty good friends?"

Chapter 4

BONNIE HAD LAST BEEN seen alive at the River Mist Café in the St. Johns Town Center. So along with my friend and former associate Alex Jepson, we went to the same café to see Bonnie's friend Nadia perform with Bonnie's old band.

Alex and I had both worked security together for the Jacksonville Sharks baseball team. But since then and throughout my last few cases, Alex had taken on a bigger role at Walsh Investigations. She laughed when I'd say she was the brains behind the operation.

But I wasn't kidding.

The River Mist was a busy place, especially for a Thursday night. It'd been two weeks to the day since Bonnie'd been found dead in the turtle pond, not far from the front door of the café and past the seating area where people gathered to eat and drink and enjoy the outdoors.

I'd hoped Nadia would be willing to talk to us, and maybe shed some light on what happened to Bonnie that night.

We sat down at a small table at the back of the café, which was small inside and really nothing more than a bar with a stage. But they threw the word *café* up on the sign to appease the town center's management.

Nadia was on the stage with a small band behind her. She was extremely attractive, wore a tight dress that clung to the shape of her body.

Alex leaned into me. "Her voice is smooth. Like chocolate."

I nodded with my eyes on Nadia as I sipped my glass of Jack Daniels.

Nadia finished the song and the band took a break. I shot back what was left in my glass, got up and headed for the stage, hoping to catch her before she disappeared.

"Nadia?" I said as I reached for her arm, just as she was about to walk through a doorway to the left of the stage.

She turned to me and pulled her arm away.

"I'm sorry," I said. "I didn't mean to startle you."

She looked past me, as if she'd looked for someone to help her.

"My name's Henry Walsh. I'm a private investigator. I didn't want to miss you, and hoped you had a few minutes to talk to me and my friend Alex."

Nadia looked toward the back corner where Alex sat waiting at the table.

Nadia turned and watched as the men from the band headed for the bar. With a hushed tone and a touch of broken English to her voice, she said, "What exactly is it you are investigating?"

I looked around the bar. "Bonnie Chapman's death."

Nadia nodded—as if she knew—and closed her eyes for a moment. She opened them and looked back toward the bar. "Let me get a drink."

I gestured toward Alex in the back corner. "How about we go sit down and order something."

A man with his dark hair greased back on his head, dressed in a glossy, purple, long-sleeved shirt unbuttoned halfway down his chest stepped in front of us. "*Nadia?*" he said, his eyes on me. "What's going on here?" He looked me up and down, his lip snarled with a look of disgust on his face. He nodded at me with his eyes right on mine. "Who is *this*?"

I stepped in front of him and we stood face-to-face.

"This is Gerard," she said with her hand on his chest to push us apart.

"Her manager. And her fiancé," he said.

Gerard was shorter than me by a few inches, but he wasn't what I'd call a small man. He had thick arms and a chest he stuck out as far as he could. He raised his chin and looked me in the eye.

I couldn't help but picture him with a rose between his teeth.

"Gerard, this is—" she stopped. "I'm sorry, what did you say your name was again?"

"It's Henry. Henry Walsh."

Nadia said, "He wants to talk about Bonnie. I agreed to have a drink with him and his, uh... his girlfriend?"

"No, not my girlfriend," I said. "She's—"

"Are you cops?" Gerard said, looking from me to Alex.

I shook my head. "No, not at all."

"He's a private investigator," Nadia said.

Gerard narrowed his eyes as he looked down at her, then slowly shifted his gaze toward Alex. His look softened a bit.

Alex had that effect on men.

Gerard said, "Who are you working for?"

"I'm not at liberty to say." I turned to Nadia, as if Gerard wasn't there. "I assume you have to get back on stage soon, so let's go have that drink."

Gerard said to Nadia, "Next set starts in eight minutes." He walked away and over to the bar where he leaned back against it and kept his eyes on us.

"This is Alex," I said as Nadia stood next to me at the table. "Alex is my partner."

Nadia extended her hand to Alex. "I'm Nadia."

Alex shook her hand and the three of us sat down together.

"Who hired you?"

I glanced at Alex and hesitated a moment before I answered. "Who hired me isn't important. But I'd like to hear anything you can share with me about Bonnie... at least before you go back on stage."

Alex leaned toward her. "You have a beautiful voice, by the way."

Nadia smiled.

I moved my chair closer to the table. "I know you didn't see anything that night, but what can you tell me about what you've heard might've happened?"

The waitress stopped over and put a White Russian down in front of Nadia. She grabbed it right away, sucked half of it down with the cocktail straw before the waitress had barely removed her hand from the glass.

"How 'bout you bring us another round?" I said.

Nadia took a deep breath—somewhat of a sigh—and shook her head, looking down into her drink. She looked up at me. "I still can't believe she's gone. I just..." She closed her eyes. "It's strange, you know?" She looked back and forth from me to Alex. "When you lose someone in your life... it's still so fresh."

I said, "Was she in any kind of trouble that you know of?"

Nadia shook her head. "No, not that I know of."

"Any enemies? Other musicians or anyone in the business you're in... maybe someone she might've had a run-in with at some point?"

Nadia shook her head. "She was so beautiful. Everybody loved Bonnie. She was always kind."

I said, "Anybody that you know of who loved her, maybe, in a different way?"

Nadia tilted her head and waited a moment. "I don't understand."

Alex said, "We're wondering if, by chance, Bonnie had a lover... if she was having an affair."

Nadia cocked her head back. "An affair? Why would you ask that? She loved her husband. Not that their marriage was perfect, but..." She turned and looked at Alex. "Love is never perfect." She sipped most of what was left in her glass through the straw.

I looked over at Gerard who now had his back to us, leaning on the bar. But he looked over his shoulder, as if he knew I was watching him.

I gave him a nod and he turned away. I said to Nadia, "Your boyfriend over there... I assume he knew Bonnie?"

Nadia nodded. "He loved her, just like everyone else. Gerard... he was so upset."

The waitress delivered another round. I held my glass in front of my chin and over the rim said, "How long have they known each other?"

"Who, Bonnie and Gerard?"

I nodded.

"Before I met him. They'd known each other for a few years."

"Personally? Or business?"

Nadia shrugged. "Both, I guess." She sipped her White Russian.

Alex said, "Do you know why Bonnie got out of the music business?"

Nadia sucked her drink through her straw, held onto it with her fingers. "She just stopped. She played piano with me a few times over the past year, but she said she'd had enough. It was time for her to move on."

"Move on and do what?" I said.

Nadia shrugged. "She never really said."

I looked past Nadia toward Gerard. "Is Gerard the one who'll help you make it to the big time?"

Nadia laughed. "Big time? I don't know about *big time*. But, yes, he said he's the person who'll help me." She leaned down and in a hushed voice said, "I don't want to play in bars like this forever."

Gerard walked our way and came up behind Nadia. "Let's go. They're waiting for you." He nodded his head to the side toward the stage. He held out his hand and helped Nadia up from her seat without saying another word.

She turned to us as she started to walk away. "Thank you for the drinks." She made her way through the crowd which had thinned out a bit since we first walked in the door. Those who remained clapped as she took the stage.

Gerard walked back toward our table and leaned down with his head next to my ear. "You want to bother her again, next time you talk to me first."

I looked up at him and raised my glass to him with a nod. "I'll try to remember that next time."

Gerard stood still for a moment before he turned and walked away. But he stopped, looked back at me and said, "We are all upset about Bonnie. Especially Nadia. She doesn't need this right now... she needs to be focused on her singing."

I held my glass up in front of me and watched him over the top of my glass. I said, "What about you, Gerard? Were you here that night?" I placed my drink down on the table, stood up and stepped toward him.

We stood face-to-face.

Nadia started singing. I took a quick look at her and saw her eyes were on me and Gerard.

"I was here," he said. "But I left early to take care of some business."

"Some business, huh?" I said, "You never came back? Not even at the end of the night? I mean... your client's on stage performing, I would think you'd at least hang around, no?"

Gerard stared back at me for a moment longer, then turned and walked between the other tables and disappeared through a door to the side of the stage.

Nadia's eyes followed him, then shifted toward mine. She closed her eyes and continued her tune... her long fingers hung off the side of the mic.

• • • • • • • • • •

At the end of the night, Nadia stepped off the stage to a standing ovation. Gerard was back and waiting for her off to the side. With the crowd still clapping, he grabbed her by the arm and led her out the door to the side of the stage.

The other members of the band all exchanged looks as they watched Nadia disappear. The drummer shrugged his shoulders, got up from his stool and headed down the steps to the bar. Music came on over the speakers to break the quiet after the clapping had stopped. The other members of the band packed up their instruments and joined the drummer at the bar.

Alex and I stood from the table.

"What was that all about?" she said.

I headed toward the bar with Alex behind me. Over my shoulder I said, "I'd guess Gerard doesn't want Nadia speaking with us tonight."

We both leaned on the bar alongside the men from the band. I nodded toward the bartender, handed him a couple of bills and—loud enough so the men could hear me—said, "Buy the band a round on me, will you?"

Each man from the band raised the glass.

"Thank you, sir."

One said, "Good luck to you."

"Cheers," said the other.

I ordered two drinks for me and Alex and turned to the short and stocky man who played the drums. He was the same man I recognized from the photo with Bonnie that James had shown me. "Does she always disappear like that?"

He shook his head and leaned forward over his drink like he was afraid somebody was going to steal it. "She'll hang around with us, have a few drinks... as long as Gerard's not around."

I said, "He doesn't always stick around, watch her 'till the end?"

The man shook his head. "He used to. Then he started taking off, coming back later in the night to pick her up. Last couple of weeks, though, he's been staying all night... watching her like a hawk."

I picked up my drink, took a sip. "Last couple of weeks?"

The man nodded. "Not sure if you'd heard, but a good friend of ours died out there. Drowned in the turtle pond at the end of the seating area."

I nodded. "I know all about it. And I understand she was quite the musician herself."

"Bonnie?" he said.

The two other band members turned from their seats and looked toward me.

"She was the best. A good person. She was a *great* musician with all the talent in the world. It surprised us all when she gave it up and just walked away."

Chapter 5

I DROVE BACK TO the St. Johns Town Center the next morning. The turtle pond was at least forty feet across and about half that wide. It was surrounded by a stone wall with ropes tied to wooden piers, three or so feet high.

Children ran around the outside of it and around all the tables as if nothing had ever happened.

There was a man in a blue, one-piece uniform. He had a long pool skimmer in his hand and reached into the pond as he cleaned debris from the water.

"Good morning," I said as I approached him from behind.

He had his back to me and didn't turn when I spoke.

"Hello?" I took a step closer and tried to make eye contact.

He reached up near his head, put the handle from the skimmer under his arm and removed earbuds from his ears. "Yes, sir?"

"Sorry to bother you." I turned, looked down into the water. It wasn't crystal clear but cleaner than I'd expected for a pond. "My name's Henry Walsh. I'm a private investigator."

The man looked back at me, unimpressed.

I said, "Are you the one who found Bonnie Chapman's body?"

He continued to skim the top of the water. He nodded. "Damn nearly fell in myself, when I saw her. Last thing you'd expect to see at five o'clock in the morning."

"Is that what time you start?"

He shrugged. "Depends how late I'm here the night before."

I looked along the stone wall that circled the pond. "Did you know it was her as soon as you looked?"

"I knew it was a body. Never expected it'd be Bonnie." He lifted his baseball cap from his head, wiped his forehead with the back of his hand and placed the hat back on his head.

"You work nights, too?" I said.

"Not often."

"What about the night before you found her, were you here late that night by any chance?"

He scratched his head, just over his ear. "No, I don't think so. Might've left around five, maybe six."

My eyes moved past all the black, metal tables with the umbrellas as I looked toward the River Mist Café. "Were you around this area before you left?"

He moved his hand around in a circle with a finger pointing down, as if he was stirring the inside of an oversized bowl. "I cover all this ground, every inch of space throughout the whole town center. Fifty-four stores. Three water fountains, plus this turtle pond. Sometimes I start here and finish on the other end or I might come in and work from the other direction. Honestly, no rhyme or reason to where I am or when."

"That's a lot to cover," I said. "You do it all alone?"

"Couple of part timers help out here and again, but they're pretty useless for the most part. There's a security guard. He walks the place after dark, actually helps out more than the lazy part-timers. He'll at least pick up a piece of trash if he sees it on the ground."

"What'd you say your name was?" I said.

"I don't think I did." He looked off for a moment. "Robert."

I looked down into the pond. "Has he ever seen anything suspicious that you know of?"

"Who?"

"The security guard?"

Robert shrugged. "I'd think if he had, he would've mentioned it... especially if he spotted a dead body in the turtle pond."

I put my hands on my hip and again glanced toward the River Mist Café. "I just meant... if he ever came across anything out of the ordinary while he's out and about?"

Robert said, "It was quiet before I left. But it always picks up later in the evening. Some nights can get a little out of control, people and kids everywhere. Depends on the band. Allen usually has his hands full with all the—"

"Allen? Is he the security guard?"

Robert nodded. "I believe he was here a little past two that night—or morning, really—and would've certainly seen something if it's happened before then."

I nodded as a kid running around the pond crashed into my leg and bounced off to the ground. He cried as his mother helped him to his feet.

She looked down at the boy. "That's why mommy told you not to run... you might've hurt the nice man."

I gave her a half-hearted smile as she walked away.

"You were still here that morning, when the police arrived?"

Robert nodded. "About five or six officers... rescue workers, firemen. Quite a commotion, as you'd expect."

"I assume they went in, searched the bottom while you were here?"

"Yes, from what I understand, found a lot of crap that shouldn't be in there: glass, coins, cigarette butts... I try to get in there and clean it a few times a year. You'd think people would be more respectful of the turtles."

I looked down toward the water. "Did she have a purse on her, that you noticed?"

Robert said, "To be honest, I didn't study the scene. I thought I'd leave that up to the cops." He gave me a suspicious look. "Can't you get the information you need from them?" Robert stuck his ear buds in his shirt pocket and went back to skimming the water at the top of the pond.

"The cops?" I said.

With his back to me, he said, "I already answered these same questions."

I heard someone say my name. I turned and heard it again.

Alex walked toward me from the far end of the courtyard, just past the entrance to the River Mist Café. She waved as I looked toward her.

Robert didn't seem to be paying much attention to me as I walked away toward Alex. "Hey," I said as she approached. I pointed with my thumb toward Robert. "He's the one who found her in the water." We walked back to where he stood.

Robert turned to me and, like most normal men, seemed to lose a breath when he saw Alex. He removed his cap and held it up in front of him with both hands under his chest. He gave Alex a nod, and brushed his sweaty head of hair to one side of his head.

"Alex works with me," I said. I turned to her. "Robert was just telling me about the morning he came in, around five. He found Bonnie's body right there in that pond."

Alex looked along the stone wall and started to walk around it, trying to avoid the kids still surrounding the area. "No blood or stains or anything?"

Robert shook his head.

I walked toward a spot I'd noticed on the top of the wall, where the color was different from the rest of the stones… as if it'd been scrubbed clean or maybe even power-washed.

"What's this spot here?" I looked over at Robert as I touched the stone with my fingers.

He shrugged. "Maybe ice cream? I'm not sure. I usually hit the stains with a power washer whenever I can. Ice cream'll dry like glue if you don't get to it right away." He looked around the pond.

I looked up and down along the buildings on either side of the seating area that stretched from the pond all the way down to the other end, right outside the entrance to the River Mist. "I don't see any ice cream shops."

Robert pointed his hand in the air. "All the way on the other side... but people come over here with the kids. Makes a mess because it's melting down their hands by the time they get here."

A group of teenagers came along and sat down on the wall just a few feet from where we stood with Robert. An older woman was with the group and approached me holding a camera out in front of her. She spoke in broken English, smiling as she spoke. "You take picture?"

I snapped a picture and handed her back the camera.

She gave me another big smile and nodded as the whole group walked away.

I turned to Robert. "What time's Allen start?"

Alex said, "Who's Allen?"

"He's a security guard we need to talk to."

Robert said, "He starts at seven. Sometimes later. Depends how much time he spends at the bar."

Chapter 6

By NINE O'CLOCK AT night, Alex and I were headed back to the St. Johns Town Center hoping to catch up with Allen Brown, the center's security guard who—according to Robert—was on duty the night before Bonnie's body was found in the pond.

It was dark when we spotted the black and white Crown Victoria, a repurposed cop's car with the lights and decals removed and replaced with the word SECURITY on either side of the car. He was parked toward the back of the parking lot, under the lights.

We parked a few spots down from the bridge that crossed over to the other half of the shopping center, with the turtle pond and the River Mist Café.

I looked in the car's window and saw a man inside, slouched down in the seat with his head back and a hat pulled down low over his eyes. I turned and gave Alex a quick look as I knocked on the driver's side window.

He didn't seem startled at all, lifted his hat from his eyes and opened the car door. He held a travel mug in his hand as he stepped outside. "Can I help you?" he said. He rubbed his eye with his free hand and put the mug on the hood of his car. He straightened out his hat and pulled his pants up on his waist as he yawned and widened his eyes as if trying to wake himself up from a deep sleep.

"Sorry, I didn't mean to interrupt your nap," I said. "My name's Henry Walsh." I tilted a nod toward Alex. "This is Alex. We're with Walsh Investigations." I looked up and down the loose-fitting uniform covering his thin, gangly body. "Are you Allen?"

He grabbed his travel mug from the hood of the car and took a sip. I picked up a strong whiff of booze floating across my nose and knew it wasn't just coffee in his mug.

He waited a moment, then gave me a brief nod. "Yeah, I'm Allen." He ducked inside his car, put the mug in the cup holder, and closed the door. "You a cop?"

I shook my head. "I'm a private investigator." I looked around the lot. "Robert thought you might be willing to talk to us."

"Robert?" he said, as if he wasn't clear who Robert was.

"Yes. I think he's head of maintenance?"

Allen nodded. "I know who he is. But... what is this all about?"

"I'm here about Bonnie Chapman's death."

Allen lifted his hat from his head and scratched his forehead with one eye closed like the light coming off the street lamp was too bright for his eyes. But he didn't respond and I wondered why.

I said, "You do know Bonnie Chapman? The woman Robert found in the pond."

"Right. Yeah, I know who you mean. I was just—" He stopped, looked at his watch. "So what is it you need?" He looked around the parking lot and toward the bridge. The crowd and sounds of music echoed off the building's exterior walls. "I gotta make my rounds."

"Are you the only security guard on duty?"

Allen let out a slight snort. "The only guard on duty? Ha... I'm the only guard... period. Seven nights a week right now." He looked down at his car. "I'm not going to feel bad taking a nap once in a while."

Alex said, "Were you here that night? Before Bonnie's body was found?"

Allen looked off for a moment. "Listen, no disrespect to either of you. But I answered a lot of questions already. Couple of officers from the sheriff's office came around right after it happened, seemed to be doing a pretty good job asking questions. So I don't think—"

"We're not with the sheriff's office. So if I can ask that you cooperate, it'll make things a hell of a lot easier on all of us."

Allen lifted his chin up high, his eyes squinted. "I'm told they haven't found any evidence to say it was anything more than an accident."

"Is that what you heard?" I said.

Allen folded his arms at his chest and stared back at me. He didn't respond.

I said, "Did you know her?"

He shrugged. "Everyone around here knew Bonnie."

"Did you see her out that night?"

He again looked at his watch and pulled up his pants by his belt. "I'm sorry, but I'm going to have to walk the property now, do my rounds..." He reached down and ducked into his car, came out with his travel mug and a flashlight. "We're not allowed to carry a firearm." He held the flashlight up like he was about to strike someone. "But this thing comes in handy once in a while. Only had to use it once, from what I remember."

Allen locked his door and turned, headed toward the wooden footbridge that went over the roadway to the other side of the center.

"Mind if we come along?" I said.

He turned and looked at us over his shoulder. With a shrug, he said, "Fine by me."

Alex and I followed behind him over the bridge.

I looked to our left, toward the River Mist Café. "Ever have trouble in there? At the River Mist?"

He shook his head. "Not normally. I guess maybe once in a while but, for the most part, it tends to be quiet over there. Especially their type of music... you don't get all the riff raff."

"What about the night before Bonnie's body was found, anything out of the ordinary going on in there? Or outside at the tables?"

Allen stopped, held the flashlight under his arm and removed his hat. He scratched his head, looked down toward the ground and put his hat back on. He looked toward the pond at the far end of the courtyard with many of the tables occupied. People were eating and drinking. Music was playing. "I'd say it was like any other night out here. Gets busy for a while, crowd thins out. What you're left with is the people who don't want to go home. They hang around out here, having their drinks. Or they hang inside at the bar. It's normally just people getting a good buzz on."

I looked down at the mug in Allen's hand.

Alex looked toward the River Mist. "You didn't see Bonnie that night?"

He nodded. "I did, earlier. She was outside, talking to some people." He nodded toward the courtyard. "Right there at those tables."

"Was it apparent she'd been drinking?"

Allen pulled a pack of gum from his pants pocket, stuck a piece in his mouth. He shrugged. "Bonnie was always into having a good time. But that night? I guess she might've looked like she'd had a few." He looked off somewhere. "She'd start

44

hugging everyone... flirting. She'd hang on this one or that one... that's when you know she might've had a little too much to drink."

"Did you see who she was with?" I said.

"I wasn't paying that much attention, but I saw this kid I'd seen around before. He wears his hair slicked back, thinks he's something special. Bonnie seemed to be flirting with him when I saw her. Although... he wasn't the only one."

"Anyone else there?"

Allen nodded. "Yeah, this girl... she used to come around when Bonnie performed at the café. But that was a while ago. I don't know who she is and, like I said, didn't pay much attention. The guy left when she showed up."

"Can you describe what she looked like?"

"Short hair, almost like a boy's haircut. She's pretty, too. I wondered what she'd look like if she grew her hair more like a girl."

Chapter 7

I WAITED ON THE porch outside James Chapman's house and rang the doorbell a second time after he didn't answer. It was early, barely seven in the morning. And I showed up unannounced.

When he finally opened the door he was wearing a white terrycloth robe—the kind you'd get in a hotel—with a cup of coffee in his hand. But he seemed almost happy to see me. "Henry? I didn't know *who* it was at my door so early in the morning."

"I hope I didn't wake you," I said. Although that was somewhat of a lie. "I had you pegged for an early riser."

"Oh, I am, I was just..." He paused. "Is everything all right? I have a meeting." He looked at his watch. "I have about an hour, not even, before I have to leave." He stepped back from the door. "Please, come in."

I walked past him. His two little dogs came around the corner, legs turning and slipping on the hardwoods, both barking until they saw it was me. They both sniffed my legs then ran away, back toward the other room.

"Come on out back," James said. "I was outside having my coffee, trying to get some work done." He walked down the hall toward the back of the house.

I followed him through the kitchen and outside to his backyard. The patio was made of cobblestones with a fireplace built into the wall that enclosed one side of the area. There was an uncovered Jacuzzi off to one side with the water bubbling inside. Two empty wine glasses sat on the edge.

James gestured toward the table. "Have a seat, I'll be right back." He turned and walked back into the house.

I sat down and looked around the yard.

James came back outside carrying a tray and placed a cup of coffee down in front of me. He put a plate of croissants in the middle of the table and a glass of orange juice down in front of me. He sat down and leaned back in his chair and crossed his bare legs. He had furry slippers on his feet, his toes exposed.

I looked past him and tried to avoid looking at what I feared James had on under his robe. Or, I should say, what he *did not* have on under his robe.

"You're here so early in the morning," he said. "Should I assume you have some news to share?"

I shook my head as I picked up the orange juice and took a sip. "It's far too early in the investigation. But I did have a chance to meet some of Bonnie's friends and acquaintances over at the River Mist Café."

"Nadia?"

I nodded. "Alex and I watched her perform, had a chance to talk with her but only for a few minutes. Her boyfriend wasn't going to let her say too much."

James rolled his eyes. "Gerard. "

"We even waited until the end of the night, see if we could finish our conversation. But he rushed her out the back door. She'd barely finished her last song."

"What'd you think?"

"What did I think?"

James nodded. "Of Nadia's performance?"

I leaned back in my chair, kept my eyes above the table. I reached for my coffee to take a sip and raised it to my mouth. Over the rim I said, "She's pretty good. Playing in a local bar like that, I guess I didn't know what to expect"

James straightened himself out and leaned forward on the table as he reached for a croissant. "Bonnie was even better. She was the real deal. I'm telling you..." He tore off a small piece of his croissant and stuck it in his mouth. "The interesting thing about that place—a so-called café in the middle of a cookie-cutter shopping center—is the talent that'd gone through there. People in the business knew the music at River Mist was always top-notch."

"People in the *business*?"

James nodded. "The music business. The owner of the place used to be a big music producer. You don't see him around there much anymore, from what I've heard... he's living on a beach in Peru. But he has friends, he turns them on to the talent."

"What about Bonnie? How come she never—"

"She had a real shot at it. After all those years and all that work. She was so close."

"What happened?"

He shrugged as he shook his head. "She realized it wasn't what she wanted."

I watched him as he looked off, across the yard.

He ripped another piece of the croissant, slipped it in his mouth, and slapped his hands together away from the table. "Aren't these croissants good? You ever get a chance, you should check out Ramona's Bakery. Picked them up for an open house yesterday, but nobody touched them."

I waited a moment while James shoved another piece of the croissant in his mouth. He chased it with a sip of coffee.

"Was Bonnie good friends with Gerard?"

James laughed. "Is that what he told you?" He wiped his mouth. "She didn't care for him as much as he'd like to think. He didn't know a thing about the business."

"But he's Nadia's manager?"

"She bit the hook. I'll admit he's a good-looking man. And, of course, Nadia fell for him. He convinced her he had all these connections. And she's yet to get anywhere, thanks to him. Bonnie tried to warn her, but... Nadia's not the brightest bulb in the chandelier."

"Have you heard they're engaged?"

"Who, Nadia and Gerard?" He stared back at me with his mouth hung open. It took him a moment to say anything. "Engaged? Are you sure?" He straightened out his robe and pulled it closed tight across his body. He crossed his legs once again. He'd dropped his slippers onto the cobblestone as his bare feet dangled in front of him.

I was a little uncomfortable with his foot close to touching my leg. So I shifted in my chair and moved it over a few inches.

"Nadia and Gerard were together at Bonnie's funeral," James said. "But I hadn't noticed a ring." He shook his head. "It's the first I'm hearing of this... it's quite a surprise."

We were both quiet for a moment. I took a sip from the glass of orange juice.

"Does your sister live around here?"

"Amanda?" He nodded. "Why?"

"I'd like to talk to her."

"About Bonnie?"

I looked back at him for a moment, curious why he'd even have to ask. "You said they were close. I figured—"

"Of course. Yes, you should talk to her. But I don't know if she'd know anything I couldn't tell you."

"Did you know she was with Bonnie that night?"

James paused with a shrug. "I'm not sure. But I don't think it's a big deal. Do you?"

"You're not surprised she wouldn't have mentioned she saw Bonnie that night?" I waited for James to respond. "If it's nothing, she would've mentioned it to you, don't you think?"

James looked down at his plate. "Who told you she was with Bonnie?"

"The security guard. He didn't know her name, but the way she described her, it sounded like it could've been Amanda."

"Was it Allen?"

I nodded. "You know him?"

"Yes, Bonnie knew him. He'd been at that job awhile." James pulled his sleeve back on his arm and looked at his watch. "I'm sorry to cut you off, but I have to get ready for my appointment." He stood up from the table.

"You don't have a problem with me talking to Amanda about this, do you?"

James looked off toward the house for a moment, then turned back to me. "She's upset about Bonnie. I just want to make sure she's okay."

"I just want to talk to her," I said. "There's nothing for you to worry about."

Chapter 8

I walked into the restaurant owned by my good friend, Billy Wu. He'd recently reopened Billy's Place, but I hadn't spent as much time there as I had when I lived at the marina.

"Where've you been?" he said as I sat down at the bar across from him. He tossed a towel over his shoulder and wiped down his hand. "I told you when you moved out to Neptune Beach we'd never see you."

"The road goes both ways," I said, giving him a look. "You should come out sometime. You can see the water from my balcony."

"Seeing it is one thing. Don't you miss being surrounded by it?" He poured a cup of coffee and put it down in front of me.

I took a sip. "I do miss living on the boat. But it's a nice change right now. I love the St. Johns, but there's something about the ocean..."

"I thought you said you'd get another boat if you could?"

"If I could afford one. But I can't. My rent sucks up most of my money. But it's short term. Who knows what the future brings."

Billy pulled the towel from his shoulder and wiped his hands. "I actually know of a boat you might want to check out."

I shrugged. "Unless it's free, I can't see being able to swing it. Plus, the fees have gone up at the marina."

Billy walked down the length of the bar and put a drink down in front of Earl, the old man sitting alone with his head down in the newspaper.

Earl had been in Florida for over thirty years, although he was born-and-raised up in New England. He'd lost some of his saltiness but, as they say, *you can take the man out of New England but you can't take New England out of the man.*

Billy stood in front of Earl. "Does your friend still have that boat he wanted to get rid of?"

Earl looked up, turned toward me and said, "Oh, hey Henry. Long time no see."

I gave him a nod. "Hey, Earl."

Billy gave me a look then repeated himself one more time. "Earl, does your friend still have that boat you said he was trying to get rid of?"

"Oh, you mean my nephew?" He nodded. "Got too many toys, including that boat. He's in the middle of a divorce, said the wife'll take it from him if he doesn't sell it." Earl took a sip of his early-morning cocktail. "If you know someone who wants it…"

Billy leaned his head my way. "Henry might, if we can persuade him to move back, get a little closer."

Earl's face got a bit distorted. He cocked his head. "Don't you live on a boat now? I thought you were over there at the marina?"

I shook my head.

Billy said, "He's living in some fancy apartment out at Neptune Beach. Living the high life, got a place overlooking the beach."

"Believe me, it's nothing fancy," I said. "Nice location, that's about it."

Earl said, "You ever go to Skip's?"

"Not as much as I did when I first moved out there, but…"

Earl said, "I used to spend some time there back in my day. Feels like a hundred years ago, which might not be too far off. Place's been there forever." He looked off for a moment. "Met my third wife there. Other than that it brings back good memories."

Billy loaded glasses up on the rack above the bar. He looked down at me. "Why don't you get his nephew's number, give him a call?"

I sipped my coffee, looked at Billy over the rim of my cup. "I'd have to wait until I wrap up the case I'm working on now before I do anything. Like I said… I like it out there."

Earl said, "He'll let it go cheap. He'll do anything to keep his soon-to-be ex-wife's hands off his toys."

Billy shrugged and looked at me. "Anytime you hear divorce, you know you can get your hands on good stuff cheap." He looked to Earl. "Is he trying to get rid of anything else?"

Earl didn't answer Billy. "The boat might need some work," he said as he got up from his stool and walked down to my end of the bar. He reached for a napkin, pulled a little black book out of his pocket and leaned on the bar. "Billy, you got a pen?"

Billy slid a pen down the bar.

Earl grabbed it and wrote on the napkin and handed it to me. "Go ahead and give him a call. It won't hurt to talk to him."

"Be nice to own the place you live in, instead of tossing rent out the door you'll never see again."

"You sound like my client," I said, my eyes on the bottles on the back wall. I looked at my watch and knew it was just a little too early for a drink.

Billy leaned on the bar with his hands, his arms spread wide from his shoulders. "The real estate agent?"

I nodded.

"How's that going? Sheriff's office still think it's an accident?"

I nodded. "It's going slow. I'm going to meet the sister this afternoon, hoping she'll be helpful."

"Whose sister?" Billy said.

"My client's. Alex and I met with a security guard from the town center, said he saw Bonnie with a couple of young kids."

"Bonnie Chapman, right? I don't think I ever heard her perform, but I know who she is."

I nodded. "The strange thing is, I think it was the sister who was with her that night. But she didn't tell anyone she was with Bonnie. So I need to ask her why."

Billy straightened out from the bar as the front door opened. A group of old ladies walked through the entrance and toward the dining area. Billy walked around the bar, grabbed enough menus for the group and walked them to a table.

Billy's Place was originally a restaurant owned by his uncle. When his uncle wanted to get out of the business, Billy bought it and turned it into a hot-spot on the St. Johns. At one time, it had been a popular place for players from the Jacksonville Sharks baseball team. But that was before the team moved to Tennessee.

Business had slowed a bit for Billy, and he thought maybe he'd sell it. This just happened to be around a time I was working on a case that involved a young man with a knack for building bombs.

One night, when Billy's restaurant was closed and, luckily, nobody was inside... a bomb exploded. It took the roof off the place and Billy's Place burned right down to the ground.

Rather than take the insurance money and go into another line of work—as he'd talked about for quite some time—Billy rebuilt his restaurant that'd been twice as busy as it was before, from open-to-close.

After Billy seated the women, he walked back behind the bar and pushed open the door to the kitchen. He yelled into the back, "*Chloe, the doors are open.*"

Chloe was his trusted bartender and waitress who not only worked for him but pretty much helped run the place.

She walked through the swinging door a moment later as she tied a smock around her waist. She had a pen sticking out from between her teeth.

"Hey Henry," she said with a smile as she walked past me toward the dining area.

"You think she knows something?" Billy said.

"Who, the sister?"

Billy nodded.

Before I could answer the bar filled with sunlight as the front door opened and Alex walked in.

She sat on the stool next to me. "Morning."

Earl looked up from his newspaper and smiled at Alex. "Now... my day is complete," he said, and gave Alex a wink.

She looked down the far end of the bar, toward Earl. "Good morning, Earl."

Billy grabbed a cup and poured hot water inside. He reached underneath the bar and pulled out a wood case and placed it up on the bar in front of Alex. He lifted open the hinged-top. "Take your pick. I just loaded it up with a new kind of tea you might like."

Alex reached inside, grabbed a tea bag and dropped it inside her cup of water. She had a folder in her hand and placed it on the bar in front of me. "I spent the early morning doing some research."

I opened the folder. "What is it?"

"Mostly articles, music reviews, local Jax columns... a lot about Bonnie. There's something in there about a record contract she turned down." She leaned in close to me. "Her friend Nadia seemed to be making her way up, too." She pulled a page from the pile. "Here's some information about Gerard. The interview was supposed to be about Bonnie. It's from about a year ago. When you read it, you'll see he mentioned Nadia more than just a few times. He called her 'up-and-coming' and said she had one of the best voices he'd ever heard."

I looked down at the paper then glanced at Alex.

She said, "I'm not sure it means anything. Because then, you see where he'll refer to Bonnie and say 'we' as if he's part of her band... or they're a team or something."

I leaned back on the stool with my arms folded at my chest. "Maybe there'd been something going on with Bonnie and Gerard?"

Alex shrugged. "Of course, that's possible. But I'm just telling you what I read. There's another one in there... a short column about how she dropped out of the music scene. There didn't seem to be much of an announcement or anything, she just stopped performing."

Chapter 9

I DROVE PAST THE Trout River Marina, heading toward Route 17 and turned to Alex. "Earl has a nephew with a boat he's trying to get rid of. I might take a look at it.

Alex gave me a look. "For what? Don't tell me you're thinking about moving back to the marina, are you? I thought you liked Neptune Beach."

I didn't answer.

She said, "You've only been in that condo, what, four or five months?"

"It's a short term lease," I said. "And who knows what'll happen. They might jack up the rent... force me to sign something long term."

Alex shook her head. "God forbid, you actually have something permanent in your life."

"What's that supposed to mean?"

She looked at me for a moment but didn't say another word about it.

I turned off the road and pulled into the Elbow Grease Car Wash. It didn't take me more than a second to spot Amanda with her nearly-shaved head. She stood just outside the exit from the automated car wash with a rag and spray bottle in her hand.

She looked toward me. I thought maybe she recognized my car from the other night when it was parked outside James's house.

Or she could've been looking at my car, wondering why someone in a beat-up Chevy Chevelle SS with two different color doors and a primed hood would need a car wash.

She watched us for a moment, then turned away and crawled inside a big SUV that just came out of the car wash. There were three others with her, each wearing the same colored t-shirt with a rag and spray bottle in their hands.

I paid the young man at the entrance.

"Nice car, dude," he said as he took my money. His hair was long—longer than mine—and he wore round, gold-rimmed glasses. In my day, you might say he looked like a hippie.

"I like your glasses... dude," I said.

I put the car in drive and drove forward toward the entrance.

"Is that the look you're going for?" Alex said.

"If I wore glasses..."

She laughed. "There are plenty of barbers around, you know."

I looked at her with a smirk, pushed the CD in the stereo and turned up the volume as the tires caught on the track and we were pulled through the car wash.

"Men at Work?" she said. "I can't remember the last time I heard them."

"I picked it up at a GoodWill." I leaned my head back. "I like being inside a car wash. It's like being in the shower... shut off from the rest of the world."

Alex laughed. "You're so deep." She leaned for the radio and turned up the volume.

· · · · ● · ● · · · ·

The light turned green at the end of the carwash. I put the car in drive, turned the corner per the instructions on the sign and stopped.

Amanda stood in front of the car, looking right back at me through the windshield. The others around her rushed toward me, opened our doors and asked us to step out. It was like a crew at a NASCAR race, the way they attacked my car with their rags and spray bottles.

Alex and I stepped off to the side, Amanda staring back at me.

"Remember me?" I said.

She nodded. "Of course. I met you at my brother's." She looked over at the car. "I recognized your car." She turned to a young man, tan skin, dark hair slicked back on his head with

61

his sleeves cut off at his shoulders to show off his well-defined biceps.

He moved the rag across the hood of my car, but didn't look to put much into it. I guess the elbow grease mentioned in the name was just a brand.

"Luis, this is Henry. He was the one I met at James's house the other night."

Luis gave me a nod with his chin, kept his eyes on me but moved inside my car with a spray bottle in his hand.

A man yelled from under the window inside a small hut we'd driven by at the entrance. "*Amanda!* More elbow... less mouth."

She turned and looked in the direction of the voice and rolled her eyes. She said, "Asshole," under her breath.

Luis stuck his head out from inside my car. "Hey man, you need your car painted? I know a kid, do you real good." He stepped out of the car. "He's my cousin. He'd do it cheap." He walked around the outside. "This car'd be nice, you get the right paint." He got back inside the car.

The man from the hut yelled out Amanda's name again.

She kneeled down and rubbed the bumper with her towel.

I leaned down toward her, my hands on my knees. "You have some time to talk?" I straightened myself out, saw Luis looking at me through the windshield from inside my car. He put his head down as soon as our eyes met.

Amanda stopped what she was doing and looked up at me. "What about?"

I glanced at Alex behind me. "I just want to ask you some questions. But, to be honest, someone saw you with Bonnie the night before they found her in the pond." I looked back in the car toward Luis.

Amanda rubbed the bumper, moved over while still on her knees and sprayed the headlights. She stopped, looked up at me. "I can meet after work, if you want." She looked toward Luis inside the car. "But we came together. Hope you don't mind if he's with me?"

I shrugged. "That's fine. Are you old enough to go to a bar?"

She stood up and put her hands on her hips. "I'm *twenty-four*."

Alex said, "Don't worry. Someday you'll be happy when people think you're younger than you really are."

The man in the hut knocked with his knuckles on the window and stuck his mouth under the opening. He yelled, "*More elbow! Less mouth!*"

I turned and looked back at him for a moment, his eyes down. I walked toward him and knocked on the glass. "Excuse me," I said.

He looked up. "Yes?"

I took a deep breath and folded my arms. "Is that how you speak to your employees in front of your customers?"

His eyes went back down to the papers in front of him.

I knocked on the glass again. "Are you the owner of this place?" I looked at the name tag on his chest—a chest that coincidentally could've been mistaken for a woman's—and

63

said, "Jared? Is that your name?" Underneath his name on the tag it said *Assistant Manager*.

He looked out through the glass at me, then stood up off a stool he was sitting on. He opened the door on the side of the small hut-like structure. I could feel the cool air from the air conditioner he enjoyed while his employees melted in the sun.

He stepped his short, wide body sideways out the door and onto the pavement in front of me. He looked up at me. "Is there something I can help you with?" He put one hand on his hip and pulled off his glasses. I wasn't sure if he wanted to fight or what could've been going through his head. "Do you have a problem, sir?"

I narrowed my eyes and looked down at him. "I do. You should respect your employees, especially in front of customers."

He leaned to his side and looked past me toward my car. "These losers don't deserve my respect. I worked my way up to assistant manager, and if they had any dignity they'd work hard and try to do the same." He turned and walked back into the hut and slammed the door behind him.

I stood and watched him for a moment, then turned and walked back to the car.

"What was that all about?" Alex said.

Luis held open the driver's side door for me and I stepped inside. I turned to Alex as she stepped into the passenger side. "I don't like bosses who act like bullies. And I don't like bad customer service." I turned over the ignition and leaned down in front of Alex so I could look out toward Amanda just outside the passenger window. "Amanda, have you ever been to Billy's Place?"

She nodded. "On the river?"

"Yes, can you meet me there?"

"Be another hour, if that's okay?" she said.

I nodded. "Perfect. We'll see you then."

I put the car in reverse and turned the front-end toward the chubby assistant manager inside the hut. I blew my horn and waited for him to look up, which he did just as I slapped the car in drive and revved the engine to make sure I had his attention.

I saw his eyes widen through the glass as I hit the gas and drove straight at the hut.

He jumped from his stool and pulled open the door. His fat, little body tumbled out onto the pavement as he rolled along the ground.

At the last second I cut the wheel hard and pulled away without hitting the building, although I wanted to. I looked up in my rearview and watched him on the ground as he tried to push himself up and get back on his feet.

Chapter 10

ALEX AND I WERE at a table just off the bar at Billy's Place when Amanda walked through the door. She sat down across from me, next to Alex, and ordered a soda from Chloe.

"Where's your boyfriend?" I said as she sat down at the table with us.

"Luis?" She shook her head. "He's not my boyfriend."

"No? The way your brother talked the other night..."

Amanda said, "James doesn't like him. I'm sure he told you that. But he's not my boyfriend."

Alex and I gave each other a look.

"It's complicated," she said.

"He didn't want to come in and join us for a drink?"

"He had somewhere to go."

Alex said, "So... you say it's complicated? Does that mean he's not your boyfriend, but he used to be? Or that you'd *like* him to be?"

Amanda looked at Alex and again shrugged. "I don't know."

"He's cute," Alex said. I assumed she was trying to loosen up Amanda a bit, because it was clear she seemed a little nervous.

My approach was different. I wanted answers. "So what's the story?" I said. "Was that you with Bonnie earlier that night or not?"

Amanda looked off toward the bar, quiet for a moment. She turned her eyes to me. "I didn't say anything because I didn't want James to know."

I said, "Not telling the sheriff's office you were with her the night before doesn't look good. You know that, right?"

"I know James wants you to find a way to prove Bonnie didn't fall in on her own. But everyone knows it was an accident. He's the only one who refuses to believe it."

I said, "Do you?"

She gave a slight tilt to her head. "Do I what?"

"Do you really believe it was an accident?"

Amanda stared back at me without saying a word for a moment.

"It was early in the night when I saw her. And she'd already been drinking. From what I could tell, she'd had quite a bit."

"Did you just happen to bump into her? A casual get-together?"

Amanda shook her head. "She wanted to talk."

"To you and Luis?"

"No, he was there before me. But he left. She told him she wanted to talk to me alone. But it was nothing. Really." She looked down and poked with her straw at the ice in her glass.

I glanced at Alex, leaned back in my chair and gripped the armrests with my hands. "If it was nothing, why'd you lie about seeing her that night? Didn't you think someone would've seen you?"

She shook her head. "I didn't lie. Nobody asked if I saw her. And I didn't want James to know, so I just kept quiet. It wouldn't have made a difference. The whole thing is bad enough as it is."

Her eyes appeared to gloss over, but she kept them down toward the table so it was hard to tell if she was starting to cry.

Alex put her hand on top of Amanda's. "Was there anything Bonnie said we should know? Was there a reason you wanted to keep your conversation from James?"

Amanda gave me a quick glance, then looked at Alex. "She told me she was leaving James. She was going to ask him for a divorce."

I scratched the side of my head. "She told you that?"

Amanda said, "I was upset. Of course. I guess you could say I was mad at her. I didn't want to know before James. I didn't want to know at all. Especially now... burdened with this secret that the woman he loved didn't love him back. And I might be the only one who knows that." She wiped a tear from her cheek with the back of her hand. "But she wanted me to know... to make sure I understood."

Alex and I sat quiet and waited for Amanda to catch her breath.

I said, "Was she seeing someone else? Is that why she wanted out of the marriage?"

Her eyes darted at mine. "*No!* She wasn't. She said she wasn't. She made that clear."

"You think she'd tell you if she was having an affair?" Alex said.

Amanda paused, thinking about it. "I don't know. Maybe. She was like my big sister. We were so close. I loved her. But James is my brother."

Chloe came around the bar and asked if we wanted another round of drinks.

"I'll have another soda," Amanda said. She smiled at Chloe.

When Chloe walked back around the bar, I looked at Amanda. "Do you know Chloe?"

Amanda shrugged, "She looks familiar."

I looked over at Chloe and she shot me a big smile as she caught my eye. I said to Amanda, "Did Bonnie say anything else to you that night? Anything else you might want to share about her and James's relationship? Or what went wrong?"

She shook her head. "All she said was they'd grown apart. And that she had been unhappy for a long time."

"Nothing else?" I said.

"Nothing else that I think is important for what you're trying to do."

I stared back at her with half a smile. "How about you let *me* decide what's important."

She looked over at Alex before she turned back to me. "She wanted to know if I thought James had ever cheated on her."

Chloe put our drinks down on the table. "Anything else?" Her eyes went right to Amanda.

"I think we're okay right now," I said. "Thanks Chloe." I looked over at Amanda. "So what'd you tell her?"

"He loved her so much. He adored her. That's why..." She looked down at the table. "That's why this is so hard. Please don't tell him anything I've told you. His heart's already broken."

I thought for a moment. "James mentioned he suspected Bonnie may have been cheating on him. Did he ever say anything like that to *you*?"

Amanda rolled her eyes and shook her head. "He's just paranoid. That might've been some of what drove Bonnie away."

I said, "You think?"

Amanda sipped her Coke and leaned back in her chair.

Alex said, "Did Bonnie tell you what she was up to the rest of that night? Assuming, like you said, you were only with her earlier?"

"I don't know what time I left, but it was still light out. She might've been meeting some friends."

"Did you see Nadia?"

"No. But this guy Gerard was hanging around outside."

I said, "You mean her fiancé?"

"Her fiancé? Really? Where'd you hear that?"

"Gerard said it. He said it right in front of her and she didn't argue against it. It was the first thing he told me after we were introduced."

Amanda nodded. "When I was leaving, I looked back at Bonnie. I was actually pretty upset when I left. Gerard went over to her table. But when I looked back, he was gone. It couldn't have been more than a minute."

"A minute that *what*, that he talked to her?"

Amanda sipped her Coke through the straw and nodded.

Alex said, "So you were pretty upset after she told you about the divorce?"

"Of course. But, really... Does anybody stay together anymore?"

Chapter 11

ALEX WALKED ALONG THE rope around the turtle pond, just as she had earlier when we'd first met Robert. "I guess I could see, if maybe you're sitting up on the rope like this..." She stepped up onto the stone wall, no more than three feet from the ground. She turned and leaned on the thick rope that ran from one pier-like footing to the next. Alex swung herself on the rope with one foot on the ground.

I nodded toward the sign. "Sign says not to sit on the rope."

Alex gave me a look. "Might cover their liability, but doesn't mean people are actually going to listen." She looked back at the pond behind her, still swinging the rope back and forth. "After a few drinks, I'm not sure she'd be able to balance on this thing." She tried to lift both feet off the ground, holding on tight to the rope with both hands. She couldn't do it.

I wrapped my hand around the rope a few feet down from Alex. "This is high enough to maybe keep a kid out. But an adult steps up here, the rope's useless." I stood in front of it, the lowest part of the rope at my waist.

"What else did they find in there with her?" Alex said.

"Her purse."

"Money?"

"She had a couple hundred dollars in cash on her. Nobody took a dime." I looked over at a young woman, yelling at a little boy for not listening to her. Although with the screechy sound of her voice... I'm not sure I could blame the kid.

"They didn't find any glasses? Did she have a drink with her? Or was there any broken glass?"

Before I could answer her, out of the corner of my eye I saw Gerard. Or at least a glimpse of the man dressed in a purple, silk-like shirt and tight green pants. He was a cross between a salsa dancer and a bull fighter. I nodded toward him and said to Alex, "Look who it is."

Alex looked up past me. We watched Gerard walk away from us and over the bridge toward the parking lot.

"Let's get the car," I said.

We headed for the parking lot, although in the opposite direction of where Gerard had gone.

"Aren't we going to follow him?" she said.

I nodded, my eyes already on my car. "We are if we hurry."

We picked up the pace and jumped in my car just as Gerard drove past us in a bright-blue BMW, heading in the direction of one of the exits.

We weren't far behind when Gerard pulled off the roadway along the front of the parking lot—still inside the town center—and parked next to a black and white Ford Crown Victoria.

"That's Allen's car," I said.

Allen and Gerard parked next to each other with their windows down. I pulled into a spot where we still had a good view. We watched both them move their cars to a couple of empty spots just off the road before the town center's exit.

I rolled down my window. "Can you hear anything?"

Alex rolled her window down and leaned her head outside. "You think they'd recognize me if I try to walk by?" She grabbed the baseball cap from on the seat between us and pulled it down over her head with both hands.

I gave her a look and a nod, approving the look.

Alex looked good in a baseball hat.

She grabbed her sunglasses from up on the dashboard and slid them on her face. She grabbed her long hair from behind her head, moved her hands around like a magician and had it tied-up behind her in three seconds.

I slouched down in my seat as she stepped out of the car. "Keep your head down."

Alex pulled her phone from her pocket, put it up against her face and gave me a nod as she closed the door behind her.

I watched her over the steering wheel. But the reflection from the sun came right at me and made it hard to see. But

I could see enough as she walked close to their cars—maybe a little too close.

Neither seemed to notice.

Allen and Gerard stood outside, Gerard with his arms flailing around as Allen stood with his eyes down toward the ground.

Alex walked toward them and leaned against another car parked five spots down from them. She pulled out her phone and acted as if she was on a call.

Gerard stopped talking for a moment, turned and looked right at her. He pulled his sunglasses off his eyes and stared at her.

"Oh shit," I said, under my breath.

He watched her for a moment, then went back to talking to Allen. I could hear his voice getting loud, but I was too far away to know what they were saying.

Both men got back in their cars and Alex walked back toward me.

I kept my eye on Gerard and he seemed to look back at Alex as she walked closer to my car.

She opened the door. "I didn't get much out of it. But I heard them say something about 'Robert.' "

"The maintenance man?"

She nodded. "That's what I assumed."

"Anything else?"

She shook her head.

I looked through the sun shining against my windshield and watched Gerard walk in a hurried pace across the lot toward us. I turned the ignition, backed out of the space and slammed down the pedal. We headed for the exit.

I looked up in the rearview.

Gerard stood with his hands on his hips and looked toward us until I turned onto Town Center Parkway. I drove slow as I turned east toward the exit where Gerard would likely be driving out of if he left the town center.

Sure enough, his blue BMW pulled out right in front of us.

Alex said, "You think he knew it was us?"

I kept my eyes on the road. "Seems that way."

I passed a couple of cars to catch up to Gerard without letting him see we were coming up behind him.

He took the ramp onto 202 west as we followed him over to 95. He pulled off at Riverside Avenue.

"Where's he going?" Alex said.

I didn't answer her. I didn't know.

Chapter 12

I GUESS ONE OF the problems trying to lay low when I drove an old Chevelle was the engine was too loud. Not to mention the repaired body with the mismatched paint and primer that made it stick out like a sore thumb.

Gerard parked his car at Memorial Park in a space along the St. Johns.

I parked far enough away where he couldn't see us. Alex and I got out and walked through a wooded area and moved from tree-to-tree to avoid being noticed.

Gerard walked along the river and stopped and leaned on the railing, facing the water. He turned and leaned with his back to it as if he knew we were there and *he* was the one watching *us*.

Alex and I crouched behind the Charles Adrian Pillars sculpture. I peeked out from behind the statue—called "Life"—and watched Gerard walking toward us. "Shit," I said. "I swear he's looking *right at us*."

Alex turned and her eyes widened as she looked over me. What followed was the all-too-familiar *click* and the pressure of what I knew was a cold muzzle pressed against the back of my head.

"Don't move a muscle," the man with the gun said.

I looked at Alex as she stood up in front of me. We both had our hands in the air.

Gerard came up behind her and she turned so we stood side-by-side, a man I couldn't see behind us and Gerard in front of us.

He shook his head. "You think you can follow me in that piece of shit car of yours... expect me not to notice?" Gerard's eyes went behind me and he gave a nod.

I turned to get a look. He was a large man with a thick chest and big arms.

I looked back at Gerard and he lifted his shirt to make sure I knew he didn't show up unarmed. He had a small pistol tucked into his waistband.

"*So why are you following me, Mr. Private Investigator?*" He widened his stance and folded his arms at his chest, doing his best to look tough like his friend behind me.

I wasn't sure which of the two dumped the bottle of cologne on himself, but it burned my nose.

"What makes you think I was following you?"

Gerard let out a slight laugh, shaking his head. His look softened as his eyes shifted to Alex. "I never forget a beautiful woman," he said. "You don't think I'd notice someone like you walk past me in that parking lot?"

Alex glanced at me out of the corner of her eye, but kept quiet.

Gerard looked past me at his friend, then shifted his eyes to mine. "Listen, my friend. I'm only going to ask you once. You'll leave Nadia alone. Don't talk to her again. Of course, you're not to follow me any longer, but I can take care of myself."

"Then why'd you bring your goon?" I turned with a look over my shoulder at the man standing behind me. I stepped toward Gerard and folded my arms. I had a couple of inches on him and stared down into his eyes. "You can threaten me all you want. I've been threatened before. But just keep in mind... I'm going to find out what happened to Bonnie. And the last person I'm going to let stop me is some small-time..." I shrugged. "I don't even know what you are. A manager for people who play in shopping center bars? Is there even a name for that profession?"

Alex looked down toward the ground and shook her head.

I felt a sharp pain just above my waist that shot straight up my spine and into my head. I was sure my kidney exploded as the man behind me drove his fist into my lower back.

Gerard smiled. "If you've never been kicked by a mule, then Ramon here can provide you with the same sensation." He nodded again at the man—Ramon—behind me. I again felt the sharp pain shoot through my body as he again drove his fist into my back.

I dropped to one knee and looked up at Gerard as he pulled his gun from his pants.

He pointed it at Alex.

"Gerard, put the gun down," I said as I looked up at him.

He looked at me with a smirk. He tucked his gun back in his pants. "Don't be a fool, Mr. Walsh."

I got up on my feet. "Do we really have to be so formal, Gerard?" I leaned back as I tried to stretch the pain from my back. "I prefer Henry. Mr. Walsh is my dad."

"I don't know what you have in mind... or if you think Nadia or I had something to do with Bonnie's death. But we were like this." He crossed two fingers together. "You don't know anything about me, yet you've followed me here for no reason at all."

I said, "Are you sure Bonnie felt the same way about you? You really believe she really trusted you with her career? You ever think you might've been the person who drove her away from her music?"

Gerard gripped his pistol in his hand, had it down by his side and with his other hand came up and drove his fist hard under my chin. The pain was sharp but quick. I heard ringing for a brief moment then felt nothing else as I hit the ground and closed my eyes.

· · · · ●· ● ·● · ·

Alex stood over me when I looked up from the ground. Next to her stood a man in uniform who tried to help me to my feet.

I couldn't really get words out of my mouth as I looked up at him. "Who are *you*?"

He didn't answer me but said, "We should call the sheriff's office."

I shifted my jaw back and forth as I tried to get my eyes to focus. I glanced at Alex. "Who is he?"

He showed me his patch on his chest. "Park security."

"He's fine," Alex said, brushing the leaves and dirt from my back.

My jaw ached. My head pounded inside. I reached behind me and touched the wound on the back of my head. I had blood on my fingers. "What the hell happened?" I looked around. "Where's Gerard?"

Alex gave a slight shake of her head with a look I assumed meant I should keep my mouth shut.

The man with the uniform said, "I really think I need to call the sheriff's office."

Alex grabbed me by the arm and pulled me away. "Come on." She looked back toward the security guard. "We'll just be on our way. There's nothing to worry about, but thank you for your help." She smiled at him as we continued toward the car. She reached into my pants pocket. "Where are your keys?"

I was a little wobbly as Alex held onto my arm to help me walk.

The guard followed us. "Maybe we should call EMS?"

I put my hand up in the air and waved. "I'm good. Thank you again."

Alex unlocked the passenger door and helped me step inside.

I looked up at her. "Did I get knocked out by Gerard?"

Alex closed the door without answering and walked around to the driver's side. She stepped in and turned the key in the ignition. With the guard standing outside her window, she tried to get the engine to start but it wouldn't.

I rolled my heavy head against the headrest and looked at Alex. "Don't flood it."

"I know how to drive," she said.

"Don't get defensive. She takes a special touch."

Alex leaned over the steering wheel as she again turned the key in the ignition. "Did you really just call your car a *she*?"

The guard was on his phone. The sky was dark and blue lights moved along the road toward the park's entrance.

"We have to get out of here," I said as I reached for the steering wheel. "Hop over me, let me drive."

Alex pushed my hand away and turned the key in the ignition.

The engine roared as she pumped the gas pedal and slapped it into reverse. She whipped the car in a circle and pulled out of the parking space.

We went right past the cops as they drove their vehicles into the park.

I looked out the back window as Alex pulled out onto the street. I said, "That's never happened before."

"What's never happened before?"

"Nobody's ever knocked me out like that." I thought for a moment. "At least not from a single punch."

She had both hands on the wheel and turned to me. "I think we should have it checked out."

"Get *what* checked out?"

"Your head. Knocked out like that, good chance you have a concussion. And you hit your head on the base of the statue when you fell. Who knows what got busted up inside."

I stared at her and shook my head. And when I did, everything began to spin. I rolled down the window for some fresh air. "Can you pull over?"

Alex looked at me, turned the wheel and pulled into a parking lot just off the street. "Are you okay?"

She stopped and I opened the door right away. I hung my feet outside as my head continued to spin. "I feel nauseous." I was sure I was going to be sick. So I leaned forward with my feet on the ground, still seated in the passenger seat.

Alex was talking, but I had no idea what she was saying. My ears were ringing. Her voice echoed.

I didn't know where I was.

Chapter 13

I OPENED MY EYES in the passenger seat with bright lights all around me. Two women in white lab coats reached in and helped me out of the car. I looked past them as they eased me into a wheelchair.

I looked up and saw the sign over their heads but all I could see were bright, blurry lights. I couldn't quite make out what the sign said.

I looked around as they wheeled me toward the building. "Where the hell am I?"

I felt a hand on my shoulder and looked behind me. Alex walked by my side as one of the women wheeled me through sliding glass doors. I was pushed into an Emergency Room lobby with a dozen or so people seated around a television.

Nobody looked happy to be there.

"We're at the Emergency Room," Alex said as she walked past me.

I nodded. "I figured that out." I looked ahead at a heavy-set woman dressed in a bright, flowered shirt.

She came up to me and smiled. "You'll be okay, Mr. Walsh."

"Call me *Henry*," I said. "My dad's Mr. Walsh."

· · · · ●· ● · · · ·

We left the ER a little after four in the morning after I argued against the Doctor's request for some expensive tests I of course declined.

As we walked down the hall, Alex said, "You should've had those tests. Otherwise you'll have no idea if—"

"I'm not going to pay for tests I don't need," I said.

"You have insurance, don't you?"

I stopped at the desk to sign some paperwork and turned to Alex. "I *pay* for health insurance. But it doesn't actually do anything. Not unless I need a lobotomy that pushes me over the twenty thousand dollar deductible... or whatever it is that'll take out of my pocket."

I rarely went to the doctor. I never got sick. And I'd like to think getting knocked out with a single punch wouldn't be a regular occurrence. So I chose not to spend half my income on health insurance that wasn't very good to begin with.

"That's the thing in our great country," I said as I glanced at the woman behind the desk. "You either have to be rich or poor. I've never been rich. But you fall somewhere in the middle, you're up shit's creek."

The woman stared back at me and handed me a stack of papers. "Call us if you have any issues."

I turned to walk away and grabbed my car keys right out of Alex's hand. "I can drive," I said. "You heard the doctor, he said it was just a lucky shot... I should be fine."

She walked alongside me toward the sliding glass exit. "I don't think that's what he said, to be honest."

I reached for my jaw.

"You should've at least gotten the X-ray," she said.

I thought for a moment. "So what exactly happened? Was it really just one punch?"

Alex shook her head. "As I already told you last time you asked, Gerard threw the first punch. The big guy behind us hit you in the head, on your way down."

We walked across the parking lot toward my car.

"Why don't you give me those keys," Alex said. "The doctor said you shouldn't drive."

I ignored her, stepped into the driver's seat and turned the key in the ignition. One try and the engine turned. I gave Alex a nod.

We left the ER and drove out to Alex's house. Both of us remained quiet for a good part of the ride.

As I pulled the car into her driveway, she put her hand on my arm. "Are you really feeling okay?"

I didn't answer, but could hear her dog, Raz, bark from inside the house. I still had pain in my jaw, but I was more embarrassed I let a punk like Gerard knock me out. He wasn't half my size but I had at least a head on him. It shouldn't have happened.

Alex opened the passenger door and stepped outside. She looked back at me. "You want to come in?"

My wrist rested on the steering wheel, I turned to her and shook my head. "I wouldn't mind my own bed tonight."

Raz's bark was muffled, but loud.

Alex said, "I've slept in your bed. It's not very comfortable. And the doctor suggested someone should stay with you." She looked up toward her house. "I gotta let Raz out before he busts through that window."

I tried to force a smile.

The truth was, I wanted to stay with Alex. But for some reason I felt it'd be best I didn't.

She stood outside the car with the door open, leaned down and looked toward me. "You should just come in. I don't want you to drive back alone."

I looked straight ahead for a moment. "I'm fine. Really."

She closed the door but the window was still open.

As she walked away, I said, "I'm going to nail him."

She stopped and looked in at me through the window. "Gerard?"

I nodded.

"Don't let it get too personal. All we know so far is he has a good punch."

I put the car in drive and leaned toward the window. "It's always personal."

• • • ●•●• • • •

I'd popped some pain pills with a shot or two of Jack Daniels to get the throb in my jaw to subside just a little. But after three or four hours of tossing and turning in my bed, I still couldn't sleep and was up with the sun.

I called James. "Did I wake you?"

He answered with a grumble. "Henry?"

"Sorry, were you awake?"

James was quiet on the other end. "Amanda was here last night. She said she met with you and Alex?"

"We talked a bit. I also bumped into Gerard."

James said, "You should be careful with him, you know. He's a little off-center. And, he's a bit of a hot-head. I'm told he was a professional boxer, back in Peru."

I rubbed my jaw. "Thanks for letting me know. I'll keep that in mind."

He said, "So did you learn anything?"

"I told him he might've been the reason Bonnie walked away from her career. Asked if it upset him enough to—"

"Where'd you hear that?"

I poured myself a cup of coffee and walked out to the balcony. "Well, I guess I was just trying to get a reaction. Although I thought you'd mentioned something along those lines."

"I *didn't* say Gerard was the reason Bonnie walked away from music."

I sipped my coffee and right away it burned inside my lip where it'd been split. Although not as bad as the Jack did a few hours earlier. I said, "Is there anything about Bonnie and Gerard I should know about?"

James spoke like he had something in his mouth. "I don't know. I guess I always wondered if maybe they were involved at one point."

"You think he was the one she might've been fooling around with?"

"No, definitely not. But that doesn't mean *nothing* ever happened"

I thought for a moment. "What if she just told you that, maybe so you wouldn't think there was something going on?" I looked out toward the ocean, the sun rising up over the water.

"She used to call him *Slick*. And not as a compliment." James sipped a drink over the phone. "But from what Bonnie would say, Gerard was more obsessed with Nadia. Maybe too much."

"What else can you tell me about this record deal Gerard was supposedly working on with Bonnie? Why didn't she want it?"

"Why didn't she want what?"

"The recording deal, or whatever they call it."

"He liked to make it sound like he had all this pull in the music industry... when the truth was he was a nobody. He still is, as far as I know."

I said, "So there wasn't really much of a deal for her to walk away from in the first place?"

"I told you, we didn't always talk about each other's business. Even if there was something to it... Bonnie was sick of the struggle, sick of trying to break out. She hit a wall."

Chapter 14

I WALKED INSIDE OLIVIO'S restaurant and approached the man at the front desk. I asked for Nadia. But he told me she hadn't shown up yet, that she must've been late.

"She's always late," he said.

I went back outside and waited in my car, parked on the street right outside the front entrance. I watched my mirrors and looked straight ahead, unsure which direction Nadia would be coming from... if she showed up at all.

I looked out my sideview on the passenger's side and saw her. She walked toward me, coming down East Bay.

I was about to step from my car but there was a knock on my window. I looked up to an officer standing outside my door.

"Good morning, officer," I said as I put down the window.

"I need you to move your vehicle from this spot," he said.

I nodded. "Yes sir. Right away." I turned the key in the ignition. But the car didn't start. The officer stood, watching me.

"Come on, you gotta get it out of here," he said.

"I know... I'm trying. Might take a moment." I turned the key again. It didn't start. I tried again and that time it started. I pulled out of the space and looked back toward the restaurant.

Nadia was gone.

As I turned the corner onto North Market a white Lexus pulled away from the curb ahead of me. The license plate said LUV-RE.

I knew it was James.

I picked up my phone and called Alex as I followed behind him.

"How're you feeling?" she said as soon as she answered.

"Perfect," I said. "But listen, I'm down at Olivio's, downtown. I came to talk to Nadia, assuming Gerard wouldn't be around. But guess who just dropped her off."

"Gerard?"

"Good guess but, no. It's James. I'm right behind him. I spoke to him on the phone a couple of hours ago. And, of course, he didn't say a word about Nadia. At least not that he'd be giving her a ride to work.

I stayed close behind James. My head still throbbed and my ears hadn't stopped ringing since I got hit. But Alex didn't need to know that. "If there's something going on with James and Nadia, why wouldn't he tell me? I mean, he wouldn't hire a private investigator if he's got something to hide. Would he? It doesn't make sense."

"You sure you saw her get out of his car?"

"Well, no. But she walked from where he was parked. It wasn't just a coincidence, if that's what you're saying."

James was on Main Street ahead of me and turned down West Union. I pulled off to the side of the street and parked. "I'm going to go back to the restaurant. No sense following him, I'll call him later."

I hung up and sat in my car for a moment before I turned it around to find a place to park. I'd had a concussion before—maybe more than once—but the feeling I had felt different. I couldn't put my finger on it, and why a good punch in the jaw would leave me feeling the way I did.

I got out and walked back into Olivio's where a man in a tuxedo—not the same man from earlier—stood with his eyes down at the front desk. He had a pen in his hand, writing something on a pad. He didn't look up at me when I walked in.

"Excuse me," I said.

He looked surprised to see me standing there in front of him. "What? How'd you get in here?"

I pointed with my thumb behind me. "The door?"

He walked past me to the door and turned the lock. "I'm sorry," he said. "But we're not open yet."

I nodded. "I'm not here to eat. I'm looking for Nadia."

He shook his head. "You just missed her." He leaned forward and in a hushed voice, said. "She had an argument with the owner. I don't know if she was fired or if she walked out. But if I had to guess... she doesn't work here anymore."

I pointed behind me. "Did she go out *that* door?"

He nodded as I turned and ran for the door. But I smashed into it, expecting it to swing outward as I ran into it.

I turned the lock and took off through the door. Outside, I stood on the sidewalk and looked both ways.

Nadia was nowhere in sight.

"Shit," I said as I thought I caught a glimpse of her.

She turned down South Liberty, about a block away.

I started to run but slowed down to a light jog. Then I eased to a fast-paced walk. My head throbbed and I squeezed my eyes trying to make the pain and ringing go away.

I pushed myself to catch her and was out of breath when I finally got to her. Between breaths, I said, "Nadia... wait."

She stopped. She looked back at me and had tears in her eyes.

"Nadia, it's Henry Walsh. We met the other night?"

She nodded and wiped her face with a tissue she had balled-up in her hand. "I know who you are." She looked past me. "Are you alone?"

I nodded. "I stopped at the restaurant... to talk to you."

She looked down toward the ground. "I no longer work there."

"I heard."

"I needed that job. I don't know what I'm going to do..."

"I'm sure there are other jobs out there... especially someone as talented as you."

She cracked a smile and shrugged. "Are there?"

I couldn't answer. The truth was, there might not've been. According to the media, the economy was humming along. But most of that was based on the stock market and Wall Street and the rich buying big houses and tank-like automobiles for a family of four. Regular people who worked regular jobs—like teachers or someone who waited tables—weren't feeling the boom of the economy. The loss of a job for someone like Nadia—although I didn't know much about her personal situation—could be a breaking point.

We continued walking down South Liberty. "What happened?"

She glanced at me. "I was late." After a brief pause she said, "Again."

"You were fired because you were late?"

She stopped and looked down toward the ground. "Ever since he tried to get me to be with him, I—"

"Be with him? You mean..."

She nodded. "He asked me to go out with him. I told him no. So he's wanted to get rid of me ever since."

I stopped. "You were fired because your boss hit on you and you rejected his offer?"

She paused, and looked me in the eye. "It's not the first time I was late. But this morning... it was not my fault. Gerard was supposed to drive me but he was gone when I woke up. I don't even know where he went."

"Do you live with him?"

She nodded. "I had my own place. But I couldn't afford the rent. So Gerard let me move in with him."

"He let you? Like he was doing you a favor?"

She didn't respond.

I said, "Was he home last night?"

"I don't know."

"Is that why James drove you to work?"

Her eyes widened. "How did you know?"

I didn't answer. "Where're you going?"

She shrugged. "I don't know." She let out a laugh—somewhat of a snort—then wiped a tear from her cheek. A diamond sparkled on her ring finger, but it was on her right hand.

We crossed the street. Nadia sat down on one of the benches along the river. She crossed one leg over the other and stared straight ahead without saying a word.

I sat down next to her. "You need a ride somewhere?"

She kept her stare straight ahead. "He's going to kill me when I tell him I lost another job."

"Another?"

She turned to me, but didn't go into the details. "All I ever wanted to do was sing and perform. Ever since I was a little girl in Argentina."

"That's where you're from? Argentina?"

"I was born in Russia. My father moved us to Argentina when I was three. When I was a teenager we moved to America."

"You've moved quite a bit."

She nodded. "Then I came to Jacksonville with my boyfriend."

"Gerard?"

Nadia looked down toward the ground, the tissue still bunched-up in her hand. "No. Another man. He left me for another woman. Then I was all alone." She looked up and smiled. "Then I met Bonnie. I was working in another restaurant and she was performing. We sat together for a while and I told her how much I loved to sing."

I watched her for a moment. She was young, but not so young where she had decades ahead of her to make it as a singer. "How long have you known her?"

"I've been here three years. I met her, I think, two-and-a-half years ago." She tucked one leg under the other as she turned to face me.

"So why do you have to work another job? You don't make decent money performing?".

She shook her head. "Not at all. Gerard tries to get me booked almost every night. But it doesn't always add up. Of course, he gets his share. We pay the rest of the band, and, well... sometimes I go home with nothing."

"But you stick with it, because you love to sing?"

"Gerard tells me people who are in the business... people who can help me get to the next level will find me. So I have to always be on stage. But I never see anyone." She held her hands out beside her with her palms facing the sky. "That's why I have to work these jobs... so I can eat."

I cleared my throat and leaned forward on the bench, my elbows rested on my knees. I turned and looked back at her. "I didn't know Jacksonville was a hotbed of music production."

"Bonnie always said it's not like it used to be."

"Then why not get out of here? What about New York? Or Nashville? I don't know much about the music business, but..."

"Pat Boone's from here, you know."

"Pat Boone? Um..."

"Have you ever heard of Rick Dees?" she said.

"Rick Dees? Name sounds familiar, but—"

"He recorded a song, *Disco Duck*." She shrugged. "That's what Gerard told me. I'd never heard of it."

"There are others, like Ronnie Van Zant, The Allman Brothers."

I said, "How about Thirty-Eight Special. They're from here, I think."

She nodded, a little more life to her expression now. "You know who Luther Dixon is?"

"He wrote songs for Elvis, didn't he?"

She smiled. "I like Elvis."

I sat back against the bench. "Did you and Bonnie ever perform together?"

She looked down as she played with the strap of her purse. She was quiet for a moment, then looked up at me. "I started out as a backup singer for her. That's all I wanted to do. I was so happy. Then she started to play piano. She liked to do that more than sing. So she'd ask me to sing more." She put a sad smile on her face. "She was such a beautiful person. She didn't want the recognition."

I watched Nadia as her eyes filled with tears.

"Do you know why she gave it all up?"

Nadia looked up at me. "We never talked about it."

I thought for a moment. "She never told you why she walked away from her music?"

She made an odd noise as she sucked in a gulp of air. She covered her mouth as tears ran down her face. Nadia stood from the bench. "I have to go." She put her purse on her shoulder and walked away.

"Nadia?" I said as I followed after her. "Do you want a ride somewhere?"

She stopped and forced a smile at me. "I don't even know where I'm going."

I stepped toward her and put my hand on the side of her arm. "Let me help you."

"I can't go back to Gerard's. When he finds out I lost my job he'll..." She stopped and looked off.

"Come with me," I said. "You can't just wander around the streets all day."

Chapter 15

My phone rang as I pulled into a parking space at the St. Johns Town Center, my eyes straight ahead at the side of the building outside the River Mist Café.

It was Alex. "I spoke to Mike," she said. "He said there's little doubt Bonnie's death was anything but an accident."

Mike Stone was Alex's friend, a detective with the Jacksonville Sheriff's Office. Mike and I had what some would call a complicated relationship. In fact if it hadn't been for Alex, I could honestly say Mike would've somehow had me behind bars, if for no other reason than he didn't like me.

I didn't like him much, either.

But we coexisted. Going all the way back to my first investigation when I was still the Director of Security for the Jacksonville Sharks, Mike and I banged heads. If I thought something was white, Mike said it was black.

But usually, in the end, we helped each other out.

Even if it hurt.

"He said Bonnie's alcohol level was two-point-one. And she also had Codeine in her blood."

"Codeine?"

"He checked the medical examiner's report."

I said, "But it's not his case, right?"

"No. Which means his access is somewhat limited."

I thought for a moment. "Just because she had a lot of alcohol in her blood—"

"And Codeine..."

"Right, but it doesn't prove her death was an accident."

Alex was quiet for a moment. "I'm only telling you what Mike said."

"It also doesn't tell us whether or not she took it herself, does it?"

"Mike said the investigator is one of the best," she said.

I laughed. "What else is he going to say? That the investigator's *just okay*?"

Alex didn't answer.

"I'm sorry, I just... I don't want to bite that hook. Mike'll do anything to make sure I stay out of their way. And you know he'd protect his buddies before he'd help me."

"That's not true. Mike does what's right. You know that, Henry."

I pushed open my car door with the phone up to my ear, looking back along the parking lot for Allen's Crown Victoria. "I gotta go. I'm hoping to catch Allen, find out what he and Gerard discussed in the parking lot."

"What makes you think he'd tell you?"

I didn't answer as I gripped my forehead with my hand, using my fingers to try and squeeze away the pain between my temples. I was quiet for a moment.

Alex said, "Henry? Are you okay?" It was as if she could see me through the phone.

"I'm fine." Although I wasn't sure there was much truth to that. I looked across the bridge toward the public area with the tables and spotted Robert. "Let me run. I'll call you later."

"What about Gerard?" she said. "What'll happen when you see him?"

I walked across the bridge, keeping an eye on Robert before he disappeared. "Nadia said Gerard was gone when she woke up. She hadn't seen him."

"Maybe he's hiding?" Alex said.

"I doubt it." Robert was fifty feet in front of me, climbing a ladder in the middle of the courtyard a few doors down from the River Mist Café. "I'll call you later." I hung up and walked toward Robert.

He was up on the ladder, changing a bulb on one of the lamps. "How are you, Robert?"

He looked down at me and squinted his eyes. He didn't respond and I had a feeling he didn't know who I was.

"It's Henry. We met the other day by the pond…"

He glanced down at me, tore a piece of black electrical tape with his teeth and nodded, but didn't say a word.

I backed away from the ladder and let him work.

The place was quiet, except for the music playing on dozens of speakers hanging from under the buildings.

Robert placed the glass lantern on the lamp and turned a couple of screws with a screwdriver. He stepped down from the ladder. "What can I do for you?"

"Do you know Gerard? Hangs around the River Mist... was friendly with Bonnie."

"Gerard?" Robert rolled his eyes. "The hot shot. Walks around like he's the boss." He nodded. "I know who he is. He's involved in the music... but I don't know exactly what he does for work. Seems to do a lot of hanging around."

"Is he friendly with Allen?"

Robert shrugged one shoulder. "You'd have to ask Allen."

I looked Robert in the eye as he turned away to fold up his ladder. "You know where he is now?"

"Allen? Not my turn to watch him. But I'm sure he'll be here. If you really need to talk to him, you might go visit his favorite watering hole."

"Where's that?"

Robert threw the ladder up over his shoulder and turned to walk away. I had to duck as he swung it around.

"He hangs at this place called The Tap, down Southside. You hear of it?"

"No, I don't think so."

"It's only about fifteen minutes from here. I don't know why he doesn't find something closer to where he lives."

I said, "Where's that?"

"Where's what?"

"Where does he live?"

"Oh, I'm not sure exactly. Westside, somewhere." He took a couple of steps in the other direction. "I'd be surprised if you don't see him at The Tap, warming up his insides before he walks around in circles all night."

Chapter 16

THE TAP WAS EXACTLY what you'd picture when you think of a hole-in-the-wall. It was tucked inside a run-down strip mall along with a shoe store, a pizza place, and fast food Chinese.

Inside The Tap was a woman behind the bar, laughing with what I assumed were the regulars, hanging at the bar in the middle of the day. But as soon as the door closed behind me things seemed to get quiet. At least for a moment.

I walked toward the bar and sat down at the first empty stool I saw. I hadn't had a drink in two days—doctor's orders—but couldn't remember how long he'd said to stay dry.

I figured it'd been long enough and ordered a Jack.

"Jack and Coke?" the bartender said as she placed a Budweiser coaster down in front of me.

"No," I said. "Just a couple of ice cubes."

"A couple? You mean, *two*?" She held up two fingers.

I looked her in the eye and nodded. "Yes, just two." I turned and looked at the other characters seated at the bar. They each looked my way, but turned toward the TV as soon as I tried to make eye contact.

The bartender placed a Jack down in front of me and walked away. She went and stood with a group of men and women bunched up at the corner of the bar. I listened in on their conversation as they discussed the Jaguars and the upcoming season.

One man said, "Nick Foles is the quarterback they needed to get to the next level. Been a long time."

"Since Brunnel," another one said.

A woman's voice said, "I loved Blake Bortles. But I don't want him throwing the football."

There were a couple of laughs and grumbles until they all went quiet again.

I caught the bartender's eye and waved her over.

She walked toward me and leaned over to wipe down the area around me.

"What's your name?" I said.

"Brianna."

I pulled a plastic straw from the glass in front of me and stuck it between my teeth. "I'm Henry. You mind if I ask you a question?"

She straightened herself up. "Sure."

"You know Allen Brown?"

Brianna nodded without hesitation. "Of course." She looked around, down toward the group at the far end of the bar. "He's usually here at this time. Actually, I'm surprised he's not. Although I guess I haven't seen him much the past week or so."

"No?"

She straightened the glass containers of salt and pepper in front of her. "Are you a friend of his?" She reached under the bar and came up with a stack of napkins, stuffed them into the plastic rack in front of me.

"I'd be lying if I said I was a friend. But I'd like to talk to him." I sipped my Jack. "Does he come in alone?"

"Usually." She walked to the beer tap and filled a couple of pints, delivered them to two old men at the far end of the bar.

She came back and said, "Allen's a loner. I don't think I've seen him come in with anyone else."

A photo on the wall behind her caught my eye. "Who's that?" I said as I nodded with my chin toward the framed pictures on the wall.

She turned and looked. "Which one?"

I pointed, although I was almost certain I knew. "Right above the tall bottle of Galliano on the end. To the right."

"Oh. That's Bonnie Chapman." With her back to me she looked up at the photo. "She used to perform here when she was younger. That's going back quite a few years, when we had a music scene."

"You knew her?"

Brianna shook her head. "We weren't friends or anything but... yeah, I knew her. Always thought she'd make it out of here, become something. She had so much talent."

I sipped my drink. And as far as I was concerned, it was just what the doctor ordered. My headache was gone for the first time in two days. I finished what was in the glass and pushed it toward Brianna.

The door opened behind me. I looked over my shoulder but it wasn't Allen, as I'd hoped. "I'll have one more when you get a moment."

Brianna grabbed the bottle from the shelf and poured me another, straight into my glass. With the metal scoop, she dropped two cubes inside my glass.

I said, "Any idea the last time she was in here?" But Brianna had already walked away, and disappeared through a swinging door.

A moment later she was back behind the bar with two white plates in her hand. Each with a hot dog and a yellow bag of potato chips. She walked around the bar and carried them out to a table toward the back or the place.

She came back and stood in front of me. "She was here a couple of months ago. A friend of hers was performing." She squinted and looked up into the air. "I forget her name..."

"Nadia?" I said.

She looked at me and nodded. "Yes, that's it. Nadia. She's very talented, although nothing like Bonnie. Not even close."

"Who was she with?"

"Bonnie?" She shrugged. "I don't know. She was with this guy. He stood out from everyone else. It was the way he dressed... like he was ready for Dancing with the Stars."

I laughed. I knew exactly who it was. The crowd in The Tap was casual... jeans or shorts and t-shirts. Not Gerard's Salsa clothes.

"Did Bonnie come in with him, do you know? Or was he here already?"

"I don't know. They were talking, might've even been arguing at one point." She paused, thinking about it. "Allen might've been in the conversation, too."

I nodded. "The slick-dressed man, his name's Gerard. And, yes, he and Allen know each other." I finished my drink and tapped the top of my glass. "Just one more, then I'm done."

She looked me in the eye as she leaned down with her elbow resting on the bar, her chin in the palm of her hand.

One of the men from down the other end called for her and she straightened up and walked away. He pushed a few bills across the bar toward her and she walked the money to the cash register. It was one of those old-fashioned ones, shiney with chrome or brass on the outside. A bell rang when she hit the button and the drawer opened.

She came back my way. "So, how do you know Bonnie?"

I looked down into my glass. "Actually, I knew her in high school. But the last time I saw her was right before we'd both moved away."

"Moved away?"

I nodded. "I know she always wanted to get out of here. I moved up to the Northeast."

"Yeah? What'd you do up there?"

I shrugged as I sipped my Jack. "I'll tell you some other time."

She turned and looked up at the photo of Bonnie. "My boss said she would have made it in the music business if she'd only stayed away."

"Away from where?"

"Jacksonville."

The door opened behind me and a flash of sunlight lit up the dark bar as the light reflected off the mirror and bottles.

I turned and watched Allen walk up to the bar. He sat two stools down from me and clearly had no idea who I was.

He didn't say much to anyone, took off his hat and hung it on the backrest of his stool.

Brianna gave me a look out of the corner of her eye and stuck a small bar glass under the Miller High Life on tap. She slid a coaster in front of Allen and placed the beer on top of it.

Allen pulled a twenty from his thick leather wallet—linked to his belt with a chain—and put it up on top of the bar.

I watched him as he picked up his beer and threw it back. He emptied the glass in one shot, left nothing but the white foam at the bottom. He burped with his fist closed in front of his mouth. "Oh, excuse me," he said under his breath, to nobody in particular.

With his elbows on the bar, he turned his head and looked at me. He narrowed his eyes. "Do I know you?"

I nodded. "Henry Walsh. We met the other night at the town center."

He stared at me for another moment, then turned his head and looked the other way.

Brianna put another beer down on the coaster in front of him. He reached for the glass and took a couple of gulps. He turned to me and said, "Any chance you're here looking for me?"

I held my eyes on him for a moment before I answered. "I might be."

He nodded with his chin at Brianna and pushed the twenty closer to her side of the bar. "Cash me out, will you."

Brianna said, "You're leaving already?"

She grabbed the twenty, turned to the register and handed him back his change.

Allen pulled out a dollar bill, dropped it on the bar and stuck the rest in his wallet. He didn't say another word, got up from his seat and turned for the door.

I shot what was left in my glass back and reached in my pocket. I pulled out a twenty and a couple of extra bills. "That cover it?"

I didn't wait for her to answer and headed for the door.

"Hope to see you again," she said just as the door closed behind me.

Allen's Crown Victoria backed out of a parking space not far from where I stood. He pulled away and out into the street with his tires squealing. Horns blew as he cut-off the oncoming cars.

I pulled my phone from my pocket and noticed I'd missed three calls from Alex. I called her back right away.

"Where are you?" she said.

"The Tap. A bar down Southside."

"What're you doing there?"

"You heard of it?"

"Of course. But why are *you* there?"

"Allen, the security guard, hangs out here. He sat down right next to me, but it didn't go so well. He took off like a bat out of hell once he knew it was me."

She was quiet for a moment.

"Bonnie used to perform here," I said. "She knew the owner."

"Did you talk to him?"

"No, just the bartender. She knew Bonnie. Her picture's actually on the wall. She said Bonnie was in here to watch Nadia perform. Gerard's been here, too." I opened my car door and stepped inside. It must've been two hundred degrees inside.

I turned the key and started to back my car out of the parking space. But I stopped. Everything around me started to spin. I turned up the AC—which didn't work great to begin with—but it only got hotter. The spinning continued. I heard Alex's voice but couldn't listen to what she was saying.

I dropped the phone from my hand, pulled my car back into the same parking space and turned off the engine. I felt myself fall to the side, toward the passenger seat. My eyes closed.

Chapter 17

I HEARD A TAPPING noise and a muffled voice that sounded like it came from inside a jar. I tried to open my eyes but I couldn't. Not right away.

There was more tapping. I heard the voice again and knew it was Alex.

"*Henry?*" she said. "Henry? *Wake up!*"

I opened my eyes and looked up at her from inside my car.

She had her face pressed against the driver's side window as she knocked against the glass.

I turned and unlocked the door.

"Henry," she said as she opened it. She had tears in her eyes as she reached in for me and helped me sit up straight.

I still hadn't said a word. I was dazed. My keys were in the ignition. I looked up through the windshield toward the building in front of me. The sign said, *The Tap*.

"I'm okay," I said as I looked around.

"You're okay? Are you kidding? What happened?"

"I... I have no idea. I guess I passed out. But I only had two or three drinks."

Alex was in a crouched position outside the car. She looked up at me as I tried to wake myself up. "You're lucky you weren't on the road."

I leaned my head back in the driver's seat. My eyes were burning. I rubbed my face with both hands. "Might've been the Jack," I said.

Alex shook her head. "I doubt it. But we need to get you to a doctor."

I looked at her and cracked a smile. "I just need to get to bed." I reached for the key in the ignition and started the engine on the first turn. "Look at that," I said to Alex. "Started right up."

"You really think I'm going to let you drive?" She stood up from her crouched position and waved her hand across her face. "You might want to have your exhaust fixed."

"It's the carburetor." I reached for the handle of the door. "I'm fine. Really. You can follow me if it'll make you feel better."

Alex stood up straight but didn't move, preventing me from closing the door. She folded her arms at her chest. "I'm not going to let you drive."

I held onto the steering wheel with both hands, ducked my head toward the open door and looked up at Alex. "Do you always have to act like you're my mother?"

She stared back at me. "Do you always have to act like a child?" She stretched her hand out toward my face. "Give me the keys."

I looked at my watch. "How long was I asleep?"

She stared down at me. "You make it sound like you laid down to take a nap. You passed out. I was here in twenty minutes when you wouldn't answer your phone." She again held her hand out toward me. "Give me the keys."

I pulled the keys from the ignition and stepped out from the driver's side. "I can hold onto them, can't I?" I walked ahead of her across the parking lot toward her Jeep. I stopped and looked back at Alex, following behind me. "Am I supposed to just leave it there?"

She smiled and put her arm around me. "Nobody's going to take it. Trust me."

· · · ● · ● · · ·

I sat on the couch in my apartment. Alex handed me a glass of water and shook a couple of generic ibuprofen from the bottle and into my hand.

She walked over to the sliding glass door and looked out toward the ocean. With her back to me, she said, "At least you have a nice view."

I looked past her toward the dark sky. "I miss the boat." I thought for a moment. "And I don't get over to see Billy as much as I used to."

"But you're closer to my house." She smiled.

I shook my head. "It's about the same distance from the marina." I took a sip of water from the glass and popped the two pills she gave me. "Earl's nephew has a boat he's looking to get rid of. And it's already docked at the marina."

Alex nodded. "You told me already." She came over and sat next to me on the couch. She put her hand on my leg. "I'm going to make an appointment with a doctor. A neurologist."

I laughed. "Why, because I don't remember I told you about the boat?"

She leaned back into the couch and stared at me for a moment. "No, it's that you've passed out twice and refuse to let a doctor check you out. And I'm sorry, but at this point... I'd say you're not okay. Who knows what happened inside that thick skull."

I scratched the side of my head. "I told you, my insurance sucks." I stood up from the couch, walked out to the balcony and leaned on the railing. I looked out toward the beach and took a deep breath. The air was warm and salty and smelled good.

Alex stood behind me. She said, "In your line of work, maybe it'd be worth upgrading your insurance."

I turned to her, crossed my arms and leaned back against the railing. "Remember, in this country... healthcare is a privilege."

We were both quiet for a moment.

"So you're not going to do *anything*? You'll just let whatever might be brewing in your head simmer... wait until something else happens?" She stepped toward me. With her arms folded she leaned into me and rested her head on my shoulder.

"The doctor said it'd take some time," I said. "That's all it is. I'm sure."

Alex lifted her head and stared at me for a moment. "You never even got an x-ray."

"Alex, I got hit in the jaw. Knocked a few screws loose. I'll be fine."

She shook her head. "You ever think maybe it's not from the punch? Maybe it was a sign you should get looked at?"

"You're being dramatic. It's nothing."

"What if you're out driving, and it's not you that gets hurt? You pass out behind the wheel and hurt someone else on the road?"

I shrugged. "Then I guess you'll have to be my chauffeur." I smiled.

Alex didn't.

My phone rang and I pulled it from my pocket. "Oh, it's Nadia." I answered the call. "Nadia?"

"Henry?" Her voice shook when she said my name. But she didn't say anything else.

"Nadia? Are you okay?"

She sniffled into the phone. "It's Gerard. He..." She went quiet again.

"Nadia? What happened? Where are you?"

"The Jacksonville Landing."

"Are you okay?"

It took her a moment, but she finally said, "I'm okay."

· · · ● · ● · ● · ·

Alex and I spotted Nadia outside on the patio of a restaurant called Shooters. She was seated at a table under an umbrella having a drink that looked like chocolate milk. She had sunglasses on and straightened them up on her face when she saw us.

We sat down with her at the table.

"Tell me what happened," I said.

Nadia looked at Alex, then back to me. She slowly pulled down her sunglasses and showed us her eyes. One was red inside with black and purple all around.

My heart started to pound. "Did Gerard do that?"

She pushed her glasses back up onto her face and looked down toward her drink. "He said I embarrassed him."

"What's that supposed to mean?" I said.

She shrugged. "The owner of the restaurant was a friend of Gerard's. He said he did me a favor getting me the job and I embarrassed him."

"The owner who hit on you?"

She nodded her head.

"So Gerard hit you?" I shook my head as I glanced at Alex out of the corner of my eye. I felt rage in my chest.

119

She picked up her glass and sipped her milk-like drink.

I said, "Is it true Gerard is a boxer?"

She nodded.

Alex said, "You need to call the cops."

Nadia looked off for a moment and stared out toward the St. Johns River. "I don't want to make this more than what it is," she said. "I need Gerard. My whole career is in his hands. And Bonnie's not here to help me... he is all I have." She sipped her drink and sat quiet for a moment.

The waitress came over with another drink for Nadia. "Here's your White Russian."

Alex ordered us each a cup of tea and waited for the waitress to walk away. She looked at Nadia. "He hit you. We have to call the cops. You can't let him—"

"*No!*" Nadia snapped. "I don't want to call the police. Please."

Chapter 18

Since Alex had insisted I drive with her for a while—at least until she could drag me to a doctor—I thought it'd be a decent time to get my car painted. At the same time, I hoped to learn a little more about Luis.

Luis met us down a long dirt road and up on a hill in an almost desert-like area with a couple of live oaks surrounded by mostly tall, dried grass for as far as I could see. Amanda sat about fifty feet away from us on a stone wall. She smoked a cigarette.

Luis crouched down low as he looked over the hood of the Chevelle. He looked up at me with a nod. "My cousin'll take care of this for you."

A black and sporty-looking car with an orange spider on the hood drove toward us and stopped. The driver stepped out.

Luis said with a nod, "Henry, this is my cousin, Renzo."

Renzo gave me a nod as he walked around the Chevelle. He ran his hand over the primed hood.

"He don't speak good English," Luis said. "But he'll do a mad job on your car."

Renzo smiled and nodded at Luis, then spoke a few words in Spanish.

Luis said, "He wants to know if you want the original factory color. It's a little more money but he wants to respect your car."

"Respect my car?" I shrugged. "I guess I hadn't put much thought into it."

Luis and Renzo went back-and-forth in Spanish for a moment. Luis turned to me and said, "Five hundred dollars. He'll paint it Dusk Blue... that's the original."

I nodded toward Renzo. "Muy bien. Gracias."

Luis said, "He'll make it real nice. You keep it or you can get more than what you paid for it if you want to sell it. I assume you didn't pay much for it?"

I shook my head. "No, not much."

Alex leaned into me and said, "You won't pay for an x-ray, but you'll pay five hundred dollars to have your car painted?"

I gave her a look but didn't respond as I handed Renzo my keys.

He tossed them to Luis and said something to him in Spanish.

Luis looked at me. "I'll drive it over to the garage." He got in the Chevelle and started the engine on the first try.

I walked over to Amanda and leaned against the wall next to her. I gave her a nod and she removed ear buds from her ears.

"Hey," she said with a nod. She crushed the cigarette out on the top of the wall. "Renzo going to take care of you?"

I looked toward my car. Luis sat in the front seat, revving the engine but hadn't moved it yet. I said, "How well do you know Nadia?"

She shrugged. "I don't know. Why?"

I gave her a look. "Well, she needs a place to stay for a little while."

Amanda stared back at me. "Does that have something to do with me?"

"I thought maybe you might have somewhere she could stay for a couple of days, until we figure something else out for her?"

She looked straight ahead. "To be honest I'm kind of bouncing around myself right now."

"I thought you had your own apartment?"

She shook her head. "I've got some friends, been crashing on their couch. I lived with Bonnie and James for a little while but since Bonnie died... I'm not really comfortable there."

I looked at the BMW Luis and Amanda showed up in, parked under a tree a few feet from where we stood. "Too weird to stay at your brother's house, but you're okay driving around in her car?"

Amanda's eyes went down toward the ground. Her feet hung as she bounced them against the wall. She pulled a piece of gum from a pack she had in her pocket and stuck it in her mouth. She held the pack toward me. "You want a piece?"

I shook my head and looked over at Alex talking to Luis through the driver's side window.

Amanda said, "Why don't you let Nadia stay with *you*?"

"That wouldn't be a good idea."

"Because you're a man? Are you afraid something'll happen?" She gave me a look with a crooked smile.

I didn't respond.

"I thought she lived with her boyfriend?"

"Gerard?" I nodded. "He's the problem."

Amanda said, "From what I know of him, he's an ass. For some reason, Bonnie liked him. I'm not sure why."

"That's not what your brother told me."

She pulled a cigarette from her pack, stuck it in her mouth and pulled out a lighter, about to light it.

I said, "Can't you wait until I leave to smoke that?"

She gave me a funny look. "Really? I can't smoke outside?"

"I have this head thing I'm dealing with. The smoke'll give me a headache. Just the smell of it..."

"Yeah? I have something else you can smoke, maybe it'll help you with that?" She gave me a wink and her crooked smile once again.

"I might have to take you up on that at some point." I looked down at the unlit cigarette in her hand. "You know they're bad for you, right?"

Amanda cocked her head. "What are you, my mother?"

I looked toward Alex for a moment, then said to Amanda. "Where is your mother, anyway? Is she still around?"

124

Amanda looked off for a moment, then looked me in the eye. "You mean, is she dead?" She shook her head. "She's out on the West coast. Left my dad when I was ten. He raised me and James." She looked down again at her feet as she kicked her heels against the wall. "I guess maybe that's why I latched onto Bonnie. She took care of me."

"Did she?"

Amanda shrugged. "She tried."

Luis waved out the window of the Chevelle and yelled out to Amanda. "*Hey, let's go!*"

Alex walked over toward me.

Amanda hopped down off the wall and looked back and forth from me to Alex. "Are you two a couple, or do you just work together?"

We both acted as if we didn't hear a thing.

"You seem like it." Amanda gave me a crooked smile. "Like an old married couple." She walked away toward the BMW parked under the tree and turned as she opened the door. "Good luck finding a place for Nadia. I hear she can be a handful." She got in the car and closed the door behind her.

Alex looked at me. "What was that all about?"

"I asked Amanda if she had a place for Nadia to stay. But it doesn't sound like she has the most stable living situation herself."

Alex said, "She could stay with *me*, you know. At least for a little while."

We started back toward Alex's Jeep. "She can't go back with Gerard, but I don't know if it'd be the best idea having her with you. We're in the middle of an investigation, and I don't think we can rule Nadia out—or anybody else—as a suspect."

Alex's phone buzzed. Before she drove off she looked at the screen. "It's a text from Mike," she said. "He said Gerard comes up clean. Nothing at all... no record. Not even a parking ticket."

"Nothing?" It was hard to believe. "But just because he's never been caught doesn't mean he's clean." I turned to Alex. "Did you tell Mike why you were asking?"

She shook her head. "I wanted to. I should have. If something happens to her..."

"It'll be up to us," I said, "to make sure he never touches her again."

Chapter 19

ALEX AND I STOOD outside apartment number 207. I knocked, and we both waited outside the door.

After a few moments the locks clicked. The door opened and Nadia stood in the doorway. Her eye looked worse than it did a day earlier. She tried to look away and covered her eye with her hand as if she was simply touching her eyebrow. "What are you doing here?"

"I guess I should ask you the same thing," I said.

Nadia looked toward the floor. "I... I had nowhere else to go."

Alex stepped toward her and tried to put her hand on Nadia's shoulder. But Nadia pulled it away. "It's not safe for you here," Alex said.

Nadia shook her head. "I'm okay. I'm safe here now." She turned and looked back inside the apartment, the door pulled closed behind her so we couldn't get a good view past her. "I made a mistake."

"A mistake?" I said.

She nodded. "What I told you about Gerard. He didn't hurt me. And I... I don't know why I told you that."

Alex and I looked at each other.

"Are you trying to tell me you were mistaken? You mistook his fist for something else and, what, walked into it?" I reached out for Nadia's hand. "Come with us, you can stay with Alex."

She pulled her hand away and turned over her shoulder, looking back into the apartment. "He's in the shower. You have to go, before he's out."

She stood in the hall and pulled the door closed behind her. The fear in her eyes was obvious.

"We came here to talk to Gerard," I said. "I didn't expect to see you here."

She shook her head. "Please. Please don't tell him anything I told you. It was my mistake. I should've never..."

Gerard yelled from inside the apartment. "*Nadia?* Where are you?"

She tried to push the door open but Gerard was on the other side. He cracked it open and stood with a towel wrapped around his waist. He looked out at me and laughed. "You here for another piece of me?"

Nadia faced me and I looked over her shoulder at Gerard. "You mean, you want to throw another lucky sucker-punch?"

Gerard squinted, staring back. His gaze moved around through the opening, looking back and forth from me to Alex. "Tell me what you are doing here."

"We need to talk," I said. I put my hands up in the air to show him I wasn't armed.

Gerard kept his stare on us for a moment, then pulled the door open.

Nadia went in ahead of us.

Alex and I stepped inside and stood in the small kitchen just inside the door.

Gerard pulled his towel tight around his waist. He wasn't afraid to show off his small, thin but muscular body. He looked at Alex, as if he wanted to make sure she was getting a look. "Let me dress." He turned and disappeared down the hall. A door closed.

Nadia said, "Can I get you a drink?" She reached for the refrigerator door and leaned down to look inside. "I don't know what he has, but—"

"We're fine, Nadia," I said. Although a stiff drink wouldn't have been bad. My nerves were frail. Even before Nadia told us he'd hit her—then changed her story—I hadn't trusted Gerard one bit. There was clearly something off with him, and now I wanted to not only get him back for what he did to me, but what I still believed he did to Nadia.

But I had to play it cool.

A door opened down the hall. Gerard walked toward us, his hair slicked back against his head. His black pants clung tight against his boney legs. He wore an orange, buttoned-down shirt with dark, vertical stripes. He looked like he worked in a burger joint from the eighties.

He wagged his finger at Nadia. "Did you offer our friends a drink?"

"She did," I said. I gave him a look.

Gerard turned to Alex. "You like wine? I have red or white."

Alex shook her head. "No, I'm fine."

He gestured for us to sit at the round table that took up half the space in the kitchen. It was covered with a white tablecloth and had four velvet-like green chairs around it. "Please, have a seat."

Gerard sat down across from me, the door at my back. "What is it you want?"

I waited a moment with my eyes right on his. "I want to know the truth about you and Bonnie."

Gerard narrowed his eyes and slowly nodded his head. He slouched with one arm on the back of the chair, the other on the table in front of him. He tapped his fingers on the table. After a moment, he said, "I don't know what you want me to tell you."

"From what I hear, you had something set up for her... some kind of music deal or contract?" I gave him a good stare. "I guess I don't understand why she'd walk away from it all the way she did."

He paused a moment before he answered. "I was her friend. We helped each other out. I had something in the works that would have put her career where it should've been." He shrugged. "I can't tell you why she walked away."

"But she did. And that's probably not a good thing for you, right?"

He held his gaze for a moment, then looked down toward the table. "She was a very talented musician... had everything she needed. Yet, she did nothing with it. I don't know, maybe she was afraid of being a star." He looked at Nadia and nodded toward her. "As I tell this one, it's not always the most talented who make it in the music business."

"So what *is* your business?" I said. "Management? Are you a promoter? A producer? I'm not sure I understand what you do or what your role was when it came to Bonnie."

Gerard looked at me but didn't answer.

"Let me ask you this," I said. "When she declined the offer, or turned down this alleged contract or deal you had set up, I imagine it had a negative impact on you, financially? Must've been bad for business."

Gerard narrowed his eyes as he looked back at me. "I like the way you work around your questions. Like a fisherman, you toss the hook, wait for the fish to sniff around the worm, then you yank the hook..."

He straightened out in his chair with both hands on the table. He rubbed his knuckles with his fingers but still hadn't answered my questions. He gave me a nod with his chin. "I'm sorry about the other night, you know. You followed me out there, and I was only protecting myself. I don't know you or what you're capable of."

I stared back at him as I rubbed my jaw. "I hear you were a fighter?"

He nodded slowly with his eyes narrowed. "At one time, yes. I started boxing in Brazil. Then I went to Peru, where I fought for a long time." He leaned back in his chair and cracked half a smile. "If there were more soft jaws like yours in the ring, maybe my career would've lasted a little longer."

I looked toward Nadia. "How about Nadia, does she have a soft jaw?" I turned to him and waited for his reaction.

He smiled, huffed out a laugh.

I said, "You think it's funny? You hit a woman and—"

Gerard pounded the table and leaned forward toward me. "You think I did that to her?" He turned to her. "Did you tell him I did that to you?" He looked back and forth from me to Alex. "I will hit a man, without a single question asked. But a woman?" He slowly shook his head. "I would not hit a woman."

Alex and I looked at each other, not sure what to think. Either Nadia really had lied or Gerard was an exceptional actor. I glanced at Nadia but she looked away.

I stood from the table and looked down at Gerard. "I find out you hurt her—or any woman—and I'll..."

"I think you know from my punch, if I were to hit her..." He shrugged, then paused. "She would be dead."

I shot Nadia a glance. "Did he hit you? Or not?"

She shook her head. "I'm sorry I lied to you. He did not."

I took a deep breath and shook my head, looking at Alex. "I don't know what I'm supposed to do here. Of course, it's not uncommon for a woman to change her story, out of fear..."

"You can believe what you'd like," Gerard said. He looked toward a clock on the wall. "I don't have much time, so if you have anything else for me..."

"Actually, while I'm here... why don't you tell me about you and Allen Brown? What'd you talk about with him, before we had our little altercation in the park."

"None of your business," he said. "Besides, I barely know the man."

We both stared at each other, nobody saying a word.

"The truth is," Gerard said, "I was just talking to him about the town center. I wanted to make sure we are all being kept safe. Especially if it's true—as you seem to indicate—that Bonnie's death wasn't an accident."

I stared back at him, looked him right in the eye. "Do you expect me to believe that?"

Gerard stood from the table. "You don't seem to believe anything I tell you, so why should either of us waste anymore time?" He walked toward the door and pulled it open. "It is time you leave. You are not the police... I don't have to answer any of your questions."

Alex and I made our way out the door. I looked back inside at Nadia. "I hear you're performing at the Landing tonight?"

She looked up at me—her eyes doing all the talking—and nodded.

Gerard gave me a nod as he started to close the door. "I hope there are no hard feelings between us?" He smirked. "Like I said, it was self defense." He closed the door behind us.

Alex turned to me as we headed for the stairs. "You think she changed her story because she's scared? What if she was trying to set him up? Make him look bad. Maybe she's trying to ensure we think Gerard's a bad guy."

I said, "Is there really any indication he's *not*?"

Chapter 20

I TOOK A SIP of coffee as I sat across the table from James at the St. Johns Town Center. I waited a moment as he fixed his tea.

"I saw you yesterday," I said.

He shifted in his chair as he glanced across the table at me. "Saw me? Where?"

"You dropped off Nadia. At Olivio's?"

James raised his cup. I noticed a bandage on the back of his hand. "Why didn't you tell me?"

"I'm telling you now."

He put his cup down on the table and folded his hands in front of his chin. "So, what'd she tell you?"

I didn't exactly answer him. "Why would you hire me and not say a word that there's something going on with you and Nadia?"

His eyes widened and he sat forward into the table. "*What?* She told you we were having an affair? *That's just not true!*"

"Then why would you have to sneak around like that, drop her off around the corner?"

"I'm telling you the truth," he said. "There's nothing between us. She needed..." He stopped for a moment, maybe to gather himself. "She called and asked for help. That's all there was to it."

"You're telling me there's nothing going on with you and Nadia?"

He shook his head. "No, never."

I leaned forward on the table. "James, are you sure? Because I assure you... I'll find out the truth whether you tell me or not."

He looked past me, toward the turtle pond down the far end of the courtyard. "Okay, it happened once."

"Once?"

He closed his eyes and put his face in his hands. "It was just a fling. We had a little fun, okay? I'm sure you know what I mean?"

"Did she see it that way? Just a fling?"

He waited, took his time before he spoke. He blew out a breath of air. "One night Nadia came over to the house looking for Bonnie. But Bonnie had gone out. I don't know what happened... maybe she forgot Nadia was coming over." He looked at me from across the table. "She could be like that sometimes... not always the most reliable person."

"Bonnie?"

James nodded. "Yes. Nadia waited for her. We sat out back and had a few drinks." James sipped his coffee. "Then, out of the blue, Nadia came on to me. I swear, I didn't ask for any of it. We weren't flirting or anything, it just happened." He twisted his shoulders as he turned in his seat. "We kissed. That was it. We heard Bonnie's car, and—"

"Did she see anything?"

"Bonnie? No." He paused. "I mean, I don't think so."

I waited a moment. "I get the feeling there's more to it?"

James nodded. "As I'm sure you'd agree, Nadia's a very beautiful woman."

"I'd have to agree."

"And her accent..."

"Okay, I get it. But when you dropped her off at work, why was she with you?"

"She called me, said she needed my help finding a place."

"Needed your help finding a place, you mean, as a real estate agent?"

"Yes. At least that's what she said. But she came onto me. We fooled around a little, but—you have to believe me—there's nothing to it."

"So that's why she was late? Because you were messing around?"

He gave a slight nod, but didn't say much else.

I sipped my coffee and sat quiet for a moment. I looked past James toward two men seated across from each other in business suits. One of them was clearly making a sales pitch, the other one appeared so bored his eyes were almost crossed. Neither one looked very comfortable with their meeting.

James said, "I'm sorry I didn't tell you. The truth is, I didn't want you to think Nadia had anything to do with Bonnie's death. She wouldn't do something like that. She's a nice person. She really is."

I thought for a moment. "Right now, everyone's a suspect. If you hadn't hired me yourself..."

I stopped as Robert walked out of the coffee shop with a metal rack in one hand and a drill in the other. I waved to him. "Hey, Robert." I gave him a nod.

He turned to me and for some reason looked happy to see me. "Hello, Mr. Detective." He nodded, "Good morning." But his eyes shifted to James—who happened to be staring down at his phone—and Robert seemed to hurry off. "I have to get something fixed," he said as he picked up his pace and almost knocked down a couple of old ladies as he disappeared around the corner.

"James?" I said as he looked up from his phone. I pointed in the direction where Robert had walked. "Do you know him?"

"Who?"

"Robert? The maintenance guy. He just walked by."

He put his phone down on the table, barely paying attention to anything else around him. "Sorry, I had to answer a text," he said. He looked around the area. "Who is he?"

"Robert. He works here. *He was just standing here with a big rack in his hands.*" I tried to control the annoyance in my voice. "He's the man who found, uh... he was here the morning they found Bonnie."

James shook his head and shrugged. "Sorry, I guess I wasn't paying attention."

I guess.

I said, "The way he looked at you... acted like he saw a ghost. He almost knocked over a couple of old women trying to get away from here."

James shrugged. "I don't know. Sometimes people recognize me from the billboards."

"And they run when they see you?"

He rolled his eyes. "Not everybody likes real estate agents."

• • • • • • • • • •

I stopped in at Billy's Place and pulled up a stool next to Alex. Billy was behind the bar and put a menu down in front of me.

Billy said, "What do you think?"

"Is this the new menu?"

Billy nodded.

I flipped it over, looked at the front and back. "New design? Or new food?"

Alex leaned toward me and pointed at the menu. "He added a section for us non-meat-eaters."

I glanced across the bar at Billy. "Didn't you already have that before? The salad section?"

Alex gave me a look as I slid the menu back toward Billy.

"I'll have a hamburger," I said.

Alex said, "Why don't you try the bean burger?"

I looked up at Billy, thought maybe for a moment she was kidding.

"You'd actually like it," he said. "Jake makes it in the back, from scratch."

I thought for a moment then shook my head. "I think I'll stick with meat."

Alex went ahead and ordered the bean burger and a salad. I added a side of fries with my burger.

Billy leaned on the bar with his hands out wide. "How's your head? Alex said you're not doing so well."

I turned to her. "You don't think I'm doing well?"

Billy said, "Well, what'd the doctor tell you?"

"That it would take some time before I felt better."

Alex said, "He hasn't been *back* to the doctor."

Billy looked down at me, pulled the towel off his shoulder and wiped his hands. "Why not? I mean, you never know. I'm sure it's nothing... sounds like this guy hit you pretty hard. But no sense in letting something like that go. Who knows, maybe it's something you need to have looked at, no?"

"Has Alex been feeding you some bad info? Trust me, it's not a tumor, if that's what you mean." I pointed toward the rack of bottles. "But I'll take a Jack, if you don't mind."

"Is that what the doctor told you to do? Drink whiskey?"

Actually, he specifically mentioned Jack Daniels."

Billy stepped away and came back with the bottle of Jack. He poured me a glass and dropped in two cubes. "You drop dead, I don't want to hear about it."

Earl—a permanent fixture at the other end of the bar—yelled over to me. "Hey Henry. Did you call my nephew yet? I told him you'd be in touch about that boat. He's anxious to get rid of it. I'd be surprised if he wants much at all for it."

I gave Earl a nod. "I haven't called him yet. But I will. I'll try him later."

Earl said, "You want to get back to the marina, this'd be a good opportunity for you."

I reached for my glass and took a sip of Jack. I put the glass down on the bar and ran my fingers through my hair, my head in my hand for a moment. I looked toward Alex and caught a glimpse of her staring at me. "What? I'm *fine*."

She let out a sigh and shook her head. "You take pleasure in acting like a mule?"

"Are you calling me an ass?"

"No, I'm calling you a mule. I would've called you an ass if that's what I meant."

"Oh."

"You're stubborn," she said. "Sometimes it's okay, but not when you put yourself in danger."

I shrugged as I took another sip of Jack. "You say it like I don't know that."

Alex said, "But now you're bordering on foolish."

Billy walked away and delivered two beers to a couple down the other end of the bar. He came back and said, "Can you just tell me why you won't go see a doctor?"

Alex said, "He claims it's because of his insurance."

"Money?" Billy said. "If it's money stopping you, then I'll give you—"

"Stop. Both of you. Okay?" I'm sure they had little doubt I was aggravated by the tone of my voice. I leaned back and looked up at the ceiling. "It's not the money. I just don't want anyone looking at my brain. What good'll it do?" I shot back whatever was left in my drink and slid the glass across the bar toward Billy. I had my eyes up on the TV. "I'll have another."

• • • • • • • • • •

Chloe came out of the kitchen with two plates in her hands. She put them down on the bar in front of me and Alex.

Chloe had worked for Billy since he bought the place. First right out of high school and she worked there to help pay her way through college. Her boyfriend was Jake, the cook in the back. Billy considered both Chloe and Jake like family, as he did me and Alex.

"Are you working in the kitchen today?" I said.

She laughed. "No, I'm actually not working. I just stopped in to see Jake. He said it was yours so I thought I'd come say hello." She walked around the bar and stood between me and Alex. She stuck her hand out between us and rested it on the bar to show us the diamond ring on her finger. "Did you hear the news?" She had a big smile on her face as she looked back and forth from me to Alex. "Jake asked me to marry him!"

Alex jumped from her seat and gave Chloe a big hug. "I'm so happy for you," she said.

I got up and hugged Chloe.

She looked back toward the kitchen and smiled. "I never thought he'd ask." She had nothing but joy on her face. "I'd like to think it'll be next year, but you'll be the first to know."

I raised my glass to her. "Congratulations."

Chloe skipped off and headed back into the kitchen.

I was about to take a bite from my burger but stopped. I looked straight ahead then turned to Alex. "Shit, I hope I'm not dead before the wedding." I turned with the burger up in front of my mouth and glanced at her out of the corner of my eye. I took a bite of my burger and tried not to smile.

I felt her staring at me and turned to her. "Relax... I'm kidding." I took another bite of my burger.

Billy stepped toward us again as he wiped a glass with the towel from his shoulder. "So what's the latest with Bonnie Chapman?"

I shrugged. "I don't know. I wish I knew more about her, but everyone who knew her can't seem to get their stories straight." I bit my burger, put my finger up in the air toward him while I chewed. "Sorry, I'm starving."

"Nobody's telling you the truth?" Billy said.

I nodded. "I just found out her husband—my client—had an affair with Bonnie's friend."

Alex said, "You don't mean Nadia, do you?"

I nodded. "I didn't tell you?"

"No. Not a word of it."

"Oh, I thought I did." I put my burger down on the plate. "Then there's Nadia's boyfriend—the one who sucker-punched me—and whatever was going on between him and Bonnie. It's a *suburban shit-show*. Everybody's full of it."

Chapter 21

ALEX AND I SAT at a table outside at the St. Johns Town Center, no more than twenty feet from the pond where Bonnie Chapman's body had been found.

On the far end of where we sat was a small stage with a band that played through most of the night. Once they announced their last song, the crowd thinned out.

We'd spotted Allen Brown and kept an eye on him for a good part of the night. Although, he didn't seem to do much of anything other than watch the band. He kept one hand in his pocket, the other holding the travel mug he'd take a sip from every minute or so.

"He hasn't left that spot all night," I said. "But we're supposed to believe he didn't see anything the night Bonnie died?"

"But it was much later," Alex said, defending him.

"I know. But the band that night would've packed up around the same time." I nodded toward Allen. "Maybe he just doesn't remember much of anything on any given night, the way he drinks from that mug."

I got up from the chair and started toward him. "Let's go see how he's doing."

Allen walked toward us with a bit of a stumble to his step. I was sure he hadn't noticed us. He would've turned and walked the other way if he had.

"Allen?" I said as we walked closer toward him.

Sure enough, he turned around as if he didn't hear his name. He hurried in the other direction with more purpose in his step than I'd seen from him all night.

We walked past the band as we followed him toward the bridge.

I called him again. "Allen, you keep running away like that, all you're doing is making me think you've got something to hide."

I ran around the back of the stage and grabbed him by the arm.

He ripped it from me. "Let go of me, man!"

I said, "Why do you keep trying to get away from me?"

"You ain't even a cop. You can't keep following me... leave me alone, will you?" He headed toward the bridge and the parking lot where he kept his car.

But I stayed with him. "You're right," I said. "I'm not a cop. That's why you have nothing to worry about. I just want to talk to you. But you keep running, you make yourself look a bit suspicious."

He stopped, still facing the other direction on the bridge. He turned and walked toward me and got in my face. "You think I had something to do with Bonnie's death? Is that why you keep following me around?"

"Well, last time we spoke you made it sound like you hardly knew her. And I think we both know that's not true."

Allen stared back at me with his eyes narrowed. He took a sip from his mug then rested it down on the top of the wall along the bridge. He folded his arms at his chest and stared back at me. "So, who cares if I knew her? We all knew her. I mean, I've been working here for five years now. I know a lot of people."

"I understand you saw Bonnie at The Tap, not too long ago?" I turned and glanced back toward the courtyard and the stage, where the band members were breaking down their instruments. One of the men seemed to be watching us, looking our way. He had a cell phone up to his ear. I leaned over and whispered into Alex's ear. "We have a spectator on the stage. Has his eyes on us."

Alex turned and looked.

I turned back to Allen. "So where's your friend, Gerard?"

He reached for his mug and took a sip. He shrugged. "He's not my friend."

"No?"

"He's just another one of those music guys, thinks he's something else. I hardly know him at all."

I said, "Then why'd you drive over the other side of the town center, huddle-up with him like you did? Looks a little suspicious, you ask me. Any chance it had something to do with what you saw the night Bonnie was killed?"

He shook his head. "Cops said it was an accident."

I turned and looked back toward the man who'd been watching us. He was gone. I looked all around and out toward the parking lot where Alex had parked the Jeep. A car was facing the Jeep with headlights shined on the side.

A moment later it backed off and drove away. Alex and I gave each other a look.

Allen said. "If you two don't mind, some of us have things to do." He turned and continued toward the parking lot.

I raised my voice to him as he walked away. "We're not done looking into this, Allen. If you've got something to hide, it might make things easier on you if you come clean."

I followed after him. "Allen, listen. We've watched you a bit. You seem to be out here, hanging around the same spot most nights. You look like you enjoy the music, too. Not a bad gig, getting paid to hang around and watch bands, look sharp in your security uniform. Yet the one night something bad happens out here, you claim you didn't see a thing? Kind of hard to believe, if you ask me."

Allen stopped at the edge of the bridge and turned to me. "You think I just sit around, listen to music all night? There's a lot of ground to cover. Whatever happened that night, I wasn't here. I didn't see a thing. You don't want to believe me, then I don't know what to tell you."

Chapter 22

ALEX PULLED THE JEEP in front of Allen's apartment building. The area was dark, although the walkway had lights along the ground. I turned to Alex as I stepped out of the Jeep. "Wait here. If Allen or anyone else shows up, call my cell." I looked at my watch as I walked away.

It was just after one in the morning.

"Make sure your phone's on," Alex said with her voice hushed as I headed toward the building.

Allen's place was on the first floor of the garden-style apartment, his door just off the end of the hallway. I wiggled the knob and pushed on the door to see how tight it was. But with a double-deadbolt, in addition to the standard lock, I knew it wouldn't be easy to break-in.

I went outside and walked around the back of the building and found his patio. I leaned against the sliding glass door and tried to see inside, but with his curtains closed there wasn't much I could see.

I pulled a screwdriver from my pocket and slipped it along the crack of the door. With one move, I popped the lock and had it open.

The first thing I noticed inside was a nasty odor. I thought maybe he had cats. Lots of them. But I didn't see any sign of one. No food bowls or litter boxes.

No cats.

I turned the corner through an open door and peeked into the bedroom. The bed was unmade. Clothes were thrown all over the floor.

I assumed he lived alone.

I walked out into the kitchen. On the counter was a basket of unopened mail. There was a laptop with sticky notes all over the top of it, phone numbers and random notes scribbled on most of them. I opened the laptop, clicked around and opened folders and random documents.

One of the folders was labeled: *Songs*. I double-clicked to open it. Inside the folder were dozens of documents. The first one I opened had a title on top, underlined and centered in bold. It read, *Don't Remember Me*.

I read what looked to be lyrics underneath the title:

You glance at me, that look, from the corner of your eye
I know you see me
My love will come as no surprise
I know you see me
I know you too well, more than you'll ever know
But you won't remember me

Although I had an acoustic guitar I played until it was lost when the boat I lived on exploded, it wasn't my place to judge Allen's talent as a songwriter. But there was something creepy about the words.

I opened some other files, took a few photos with my phone, then opened another folder with photos inside. Inside were hundreds or even thousands of images. Many were photographs of bands, most I didn't recognize. I continued to click and see if anything caught my eye.

And something did.

There were dozens of photos of Bonnie Chapman. Some were of her performing on stage. But there were plenty where she wasn't in her act. They weren't all perfect or sharp. Some were somewhat distorted and appeared to be shot from a distance with a telephoto lens.

Some photos looked like they all took place at the same time in the same location, with Bonnie sitting or standing or in the middle of a conversation. One caught my eye, her eyes coming straight at the camera as if she spotted Allen—or whoever it was—taking her photo. As I looked at the screen, it was as if Bonnie looked out at me right from the computer.

There were other photos. Some of Nadia, but mostly of her performing on stage.

I took pictures of the photos on the computer. But they didn't come out very clear. And I knew it would take all night to capture every image I wanted. I was about to take another when my phone buzzed in my hand. It was Alex.

"Yeah?" I said.

"You gotta get out of there. An officer just arrived, walking up the walkway."

"Did he see you?"

Alex said, "It's a *she*. But, no, I don't think so. She parked a few spots down from me."

I hurried across the apartment to the sliding glass door, the phone still up to my ear as I stepped out onto the patio. "Someone must've called the cops," I said. "Why don't you drive around back, I'll cut through the woods and meet you back there, on the street."

As soon as I stepped off the patio, a flashlight shined directly into my eyes. It was hard to see, but I knew who it was.

"Hands up where I can see them," she said.

I raised my hands up just over my shoulders. "Officer. Hi, I'm glad to see you. My ID is in my back pocket if you just—"

"Sir, stop talking. What are you doing back here at this time of night?"

I looked at the gun in her hands. "I'm just leaving my friend's, on my way home."

She looked past me, toward the sliding glass door. "Who's your friend?"

I started to lower my hands.

"Keep them up," she said.

"Allen Brown."

"Is he inside?"

I hesitated a moment before I answered. "No, he's not."

"Then why are you here if Mr. Brown isn't inside? And why are you leaving through his back door?"

I put my index finger up and slowly moved my hand down toward my pants. "Let me get you my ID. My name is Henry Walsh. I'm a private investigator."

"*Keep your hands up!*" she snapped.

"I was going to show you my ID."

She turned the light off on her gun and gave me a nod as she clicked on the two-way clipped to her vest. "Location, Jax Atlantic Apartments. Possible ten-sixty-two, suspect present. Backup requested."

She tucked her gun in her holster. "Hands on top of your head."

"What? But I'm—"

"Hands on top of your head, sir."

I did as she asked.

She grabbed one arm at a time and slapped the cuffs on my wrists.

I didn't resist.

She held onto my wrists and tugged me along as we walked together across the patio outside Allen's apartment. She pulled on the glass door and poked her head inside. "What were you doing in this man's apartment?"

"I'm a private investigator. My license is in my wallet."

"Are you here alone?" She reached around for my wallet and opened it.

"Yes, I'm here alone," I said.

"Who was that you were talking to on the phone?"

I said, "Oh, that? I don't know. I was just—"

She pulled me by the arm and walked me off the patio, away from Allen's apartment.

I said, "I actually walked here. My car's being painted."

She appeared to have had enough, and pulled me without another word until we got to her cruiser. The officer opened the back door, pushed my head down and eased me inside, closing the door behind me.

A second cruiser pulled up behind us and I looked out the window and wondered where Alex had gone. I knew she was probably watching me from wherever she was. I'd hoped maybe she got one of her friends on the horn.

I sat in the backseat with my hands cuffed behind my back for at least thirty minutes, maybe more, when the officer finally opened my door. "Mr. Walsh?" she said. "This is your lucky day." She pulled me from the car, turned me around and removed the handcuffs from my wrists. "If it were up to me, you'd spend the night on the cold floor of a jail cell." She clipped the cuffs on the back of her belt. "But it's not up to me. So you're free to go."

"Thank you," I said. "I was just doing my job. Like *you* were."

She gave me a look and shook her head. "I didn't break the law. You can't just walk into a man's private residence like that."

I nodded and kept my mouth shut.

Both officers got back in their cars and drove away. I stood alone on the sidewalk as I watched their tail lights disappear around the corner.

Just as I pulled my phone from my pocket, about to call Alex, headlights shined on me. I wondered why she came toward me from the other direction.

The lights became brighter as the car—or Jeep—got closer. And by the time it was right on top of me, I realized it wasn't Alex.

A light rain started to fall as I heard the doors open and close from behind the headlights. I couldn't see well enough to know who it was.

Two figures walk toward me.

Before I could even say a word I felt a crack on my back. I fell to the ground and was immediately lifted to my feet by the two men from the car. Nobody spoke a word as the third man behind me—the one I couldn't see coming—punched me hard in the back of my ribs.

The two men wore ski masks. When I turned to look at whoever was behind me I again felt another crack against my back. I dropped to one knee. One of the two masked men had me by the arm with a baseball bat in his hand.

But for a split second he loosened his grip. That's when I came up with a punch that landed under his chin. He was knocked off his feet and thrown backwards onto the hood of the car. The bat fell from his hands and bounced on the road.

The man behind me threw a punch into the back of my head. I dropped down toward the ground and picked up the bat, came up with a wild swing and struck the second man from the car. He was short and wide and didn't go down at first.

So I took another swing and he spun around then dropped on top of his friend.

Tires squealed from around the curve in the road. Bright headlights came up the street toward us. Just as the man I'd struck with the bat tried to come to his feet, Alex drove by in the Jeep and leaned out with a thick, long flashlight in her hand. She swung it at the man and caught him in the face.

He dropped right down to the ground.

I turned and got a look at the last man standing—the one who'd hit me with something from behind—and spun the bat in my hand like a hitter walking to the plate.

He backpedaled as I stepped toward him and came out with a gun in his hand. He didn't say a word.

But Alex had already stopped and jumped from the Jeep. She came up behind him with her Glock pointed at the back of his head. "Drop it," she said.

He turned with his gun but before he could do a thing I swung the bat and knocked his piece from his hand. It bounced off the sidewalk and into the wet grass.

I took another swing... going for the cycle.

With one swing he was down on his back.

Good night.

"Get in," Alex said as we both ran for the Jeep. She hit the gas hard. Her tires spun underneath on the wet pavement. The rain came down hard.

I hung out the passenger side of the Jeep and looked back toward the men as they stumbled and tried to get to their feet.

Chapter 23

ALEX TURNED TO ME from behind the wheel of her Jeep, on our way out to pick up my car. "I know you're excited to get your car back," she said, "but I think it makes sense to give it some time before you drive. I'm sure the doctor would say the same thing."

"I have to drive it home, don't I?"

She nodded. "I'll follow you back to Neptune Beach, park it and I'll take you wherever you need to go." She gave me a quick look. "You're lucky you made it out of Allen's apartment alive, you know."

"Make sure you thank Mike for me, too. I wasn't looking forward to a night behind bars."

Alex kept her eyes on the road, quiet for a couple of moments. "I woke up wishing we'd grabbed one of them."

"Last night?" I stared back at her. "I thought the same thing. I didn't even get a plate."

Alex said, "We should show those pictures you took to Mike."

I shook my head as I looked at her from the passenger seat. "What good'll that do?"

"Well, there's a security guard who spends his nights drinking booze from a travel mug, and appears he might—at the very least—be a stalker."

"I don't know. Just because he took pictures of Bonnie..."

Alex turned the Jeep down the dirt road as dust flew up all around us from under the wheels. We bounced up and down in our seats as we hit the dips and holes in the so-called road.

Up ahead was the garage where Luis's cousin ran his business. It was an old building with a blue steel exterior, stained with streaks of rust.

Amanda's BMW—the one she'd inherited from Bonnie—was parked out front. Amanda sat next to the garage door in a gray folding chair. She had a cigarette in her hand but tossed it as we drove toward her. She stood as Alex parked the Jeep behind the BMW.

She smiled. "Wait till you see it," she said as she stepped into the open garage. "*Renzo!*" she yelled. "*Henry's here for his car.*"

Renzo walked out a moment later as he wiped his hands with a red rag. He gave me a nod with his chin as he glanced at Amanda, but didn't say a word before he stuck two fingers in his mouth and made a loud whistle.

A young man ran toward him from inside the garage. Renzo said something to him in Spanish before he turned and ran back inside.

A moment later I heard the Chevelle's engine. The young man drove it out from the garage and parked it next to the Jeep as I stepped aside and admired Renzo's work. I barely recognized my car. The primed hood and the mismatched doors were gone.

It was painted a sharp blue, like the ones you'd see in muscle car magazines. I didn't know enough about the car to say whether or not it was the original factory-finished blue, as Renzo had first claimed.

But I didn't care. It looked good.

"Whachu think?" Renzo said.

I tilted my head. "You speak English?"

He shrugged and nodded. Maybe he only knew a few words.

I turned to Amanda. "Where's Luis?"

She didn't answer, but exchanged a look with Renzo.

I pulled open the door and looked inside, then glanced back at Renzo. "You even cleaned inside?"

He nodded and held his hand over his eyes to shade them from the sun rising up over the hill.

I reached into my pocket and handed him an envelope with cash. He didn't open it or count the money, but stuck it in his shirt pocket. He reached out and shook my hand.

• • • • • • • • • •

160

Somehow I convinced Alex to let me drive. I'd felt better, and at the time could only hope I was perhaps past the blackouts.

For someone who was never much of a *car guy*, I liked driving a car that had just a few days ago looked like it was ready for the salvage yard. I turned to Alex as she stared straight ahead toward the road, the wind blowing her hair straight back behind her seat. I had the engine running hard. "Runs good, doesn't it?"

She turned to me and nodded, but I could tell she didn't share my excitement.

I said, "You ever notice when you clean your car—or get it painted—the engine seems to run better?"

She shook her head. "Not really."

I gave her a look. "Something wrong?"

"What do you think is wrong? I'm nervous with you behind the wheel. And you're acting like everything's fine inside that thick skull of yours. And it's not."

I rolled my eyes but didn't say another word, my eyes ahead on the road.

We were southbound on 295 and I turned hard as the tired squealed and I jumped onto the ramp for Town Center Parkway.

Alex gripped the handle on the door with one hand, the other against the dashboard. "I thought we were going to see James?"

"We are," I said. "I want to stop by and talk to Robert."

I pulled into the lot just behind the pond. "I get the feeling Robert's got a thing about keeping his mouth shut. I'm not sure he wants to be involved in any of this"

We walked around the pond and into the courtyard. There were plenty of people seated outside at the tables, enjoying the morning under the umbrellas before the sun got too hot.

We walked inside the Coffee Bean, ordered a coffee for me and a tea for Alex from the young man with quite a few earrings attached to his face. He wore large, round glasses with dark rims. Something you'd see on an old woman. The side of his neck had a tattoo of a hand, as if it'd wrapped around him with a grip on his throat.

"That all?" he said as he tapped the keys on the register.

I handed him a couple of bills. "Is Robert around by any chance?"

He looked up but didn't exactly make eye contact. "Robert?"

"I thought maybe you knew him. He's the head of maintenance here at the town center. He fixes things... I'm sure you'd know him if you saw him?"

He shrugged and handed me my change, his eyes still down as if making eye contact would give him hives.

"No idea?" I said.

He looked up, but his eyes went to Alex. "Oh, Roberto?"

"Roberto?"

He shrugged again, cracked half a smile. "I call him Roberto. I think he's Mexican or something, isn't he?"

I thought about it. "I don't think he is. Not even close, in fact." I said to the kid, "So have you seen him around?"

The smile—more of a smirk—dropped from the kid's face. He turned to a young woman at the sink behind him. "Hey, have you seen Roberto?"

She looked at us over her shoulder, shaking her head. "I've been calling him all morning. The sink's backed up again." She pulled a paper towel from the dispenser and turned to us, wiping her hands. "He usually calls right back when we need him."

"How long have you been calling him?" I said.

She looked up at the clock on the wall. "Since seven."

I looked up at the clock. "You have his number?"

She turned and stepped toward a cork board, removed a tack and pulled down a business card. She handed it to me. "If you talk to him, tell him to come fix our sink right away before we have another flood."

I looked down at the card and stuck it in my pocket. "Sure, I'll tell him that. Thanks." I gave Alex a look and we both walked outside.

Chapter 24

I CALLED ROBERT'S PHONE on our way to James's house but he never answered. In fact it didn't even ring, went right to voicemail each time I tried. I didn't leave a message.

"Maybe he's sick," Alex said.

I shrugged. "Maybe."

We pulled into the circular driveway in front of James's house and parked behind his Lexus. The top was down.

James was in the doorway with his eyes down on his phone. "I thought you said you'd be here a half hour ago."

"Sorry," I said. "Had to make a stop by the town center."

James smiled at Alex—stared at her, actually—until he turned around and walked back into the house.

We followed him inside, down the hall and through the kitchen. We walked out the door to his backyard where he had a basket of muffins, a pitcher of orange juice, and a carafe of coffee on the table.

Quite the host.

As we sat down, James poured us each a cup of coffee in small cups made of china. I felt I should perhaps stick my pinkie in the air when I took a sip.

"I have to leave in forty-five," James said.

"Do you have a showing?" I said, as if I was interested in hearing about his real estate business.

He looked down at himself, dressed in a pair of khaki slacks and a pink golf shirt. He shook his head. "I'm playing eighteen." He crossed his legs, sipped from his cup and looked at me over the rim. "So what do you have? I hope you've made progress?"

I reached for the pitcher of orange juice and poured myself a glass. I didn't answer his specific question. "Did Bonnie ever mention someone by the name of Allen Brown?"

James put his cup down on the table. He looked back at me for a moment, his eyes squinted. "Allen Brown?" He chewed the inside of his cheek and slowly shook his head. He placed one hand over the other on top of his knee. "The name doesn't ring a bell."

"He's a security guard at the St. Johns Town Center."

James picked up his cup and took a sip. His pinkie stuck straight out the side. "Maybe Bonnie knew him? I don't know. Where would I have heard the name? It's not like I hang out at the town center very often."

Alex said, "You must've watched Bonnie perform at the town center?"

He turned to her, then let his eyes move past us. He stared off for a moment, almost in a daze. He shrugged. "I guess..." He looked right at me. "Actually, no. I didn't." He paused, quiet again for another moment, like his mind was somewhere else. "Something I've come to regret, in hindsight. Although that's just how we were. We each did our own thing." He focused on Alex and shook his head. "I didn't watch her perform as often as I wish I had. Especially the last couple of years."

I leaned back in my chair and turned, gave Alex a look. I said to James, "Allen Brown seemed to be a fan of Bonnie's."

"Most people were."

I sipped my coffee. "He might be a little more of a fan than the others. I found some images on his computer. He had a lot of photos of Bonnie."

James waited, not saying a word.

"It doesn't mean he had anything to do with her death, or that he's committed any crimes. but..."

"What were the pictures of?" James said.

"Mostly on stage, of Bonnie performing. Some of when she was younger, from what I could tell. So taking her picture wasn't some new hobby of his."

Alex said, "Keep in mind, he could just be an amateur photographer who enjoyed music."

"The photos weren't just of Bonnie, either. There were some of Nadia, and photos of other musicians."

James sat back in his chair. "Did you talk to him?"

I picked up the OJ and took another sip. "I spoke with him a couple of times. But I never mentioned the photos. Of course, he doesn't know I was in his apartment—at least not that I know of—but we're looking into it. That's why I stopped at the town center on our way here. Wanted to talk to Robert, the man I asked you about... the maintenance man."

James squinted. "You said his name's Robert, right?" James scratched his head. I was thinking about it, after you said we saw him." He paused a moment. "I don't know if it's the same guy, but we had someone come over here and do some work around the house. It was some time ago. Might've done some electrical work. Bonnie knew him from the town center."

"He's the same man I told you took off in the other direction after he looked at you."

James shrugged. "Like I'd said, I didn't see him. I don't know, maybe it's him... maybe not."

I said, "But you're sure it was someone from the town center who came over, did some work?"

James nodded. "Bonnie was always helping people out. She'd find work for someone, help put a little extra money in their pockets. I bet there'd been a dozen different people here over the years, doing odd jobs around the house."

I said, "Did you mention any of this to the sheriff's office?"

James shrugged. "I'm mentioning it now."

"We're not the cops," I said.

He shrugged again and shook his head. "I rarely paid attention to who was coming and going. I'm busy, you know."

James broke off a piece of muffin and stuck it in his mouth. He wiped his hands with the cloth napkin from his lap. "So what about this gentleman... Robert? Is he a suspect? Or is he someone who might know something about the security guard?"

I said, "I need to talk to him. I've been trying to reach him, but he doesn't answer his phone. I mean, I don't know if he knows much about Allen, to be honest. They don't seem to be friends or anything." I took another sip of coffee and stood from the table. "James, do me a favor. If you think of anything else at all... anything about this man Allen or Robert or anyone else who might've been around here or around Bonnie... make sure you give me a call."

James got up from the table and walked us through the house and out the front door.

"Henry," he said as I walked past him toward the car.

I turned.

"This man, Allen, was there anything else about him? The more I think about it... his name seems familiar. I don't know... something about him."

I stood by my car and looked back at James, his eyes down toward the driveway. "There was music on his computer," I said. "Words... It looks like he wrote songs. Love songs."

James turned without saying a word and walked back into the house.

Alex and I both looked at each other across the roof of the car, then walked back toward the house.

The door opened and James walked outside with a stack of envelopes in his hands as he flipped through each one. "There's no return address," he said. He handed half the stack to me.

The envelopes were addressed to Bonnie.

"Someone used to mail songs to her," he said. "Bonnie never said who it was."

"Because she didn't know? Or because she didn't tell you?"

James said. "I guess I can't answer that."

Chapter 25

NADIA AND HER BAND tuned up on stage when Alex and I showed up at The Jacksonville Landing. She turned and walked toward us with her big sunglasses on her face, even though the sunlight had started to fade.

"Where's Gerard?" I said when she stopped in front of me and Alex.

She looked past us, out toward the crowd. "He'll be back... hopefully before the show starts."

I looked around. "Pretty good turnout," I said.

Nadia swallowed hard. "I've never performed in front of so many people. At least not alone."

"You're not nervous, *are* you?" Alex said.

She shrugged. "I wish Bonnie were here. She'd help me re-lax."

"We've heard you sing," Alex said. "You have nothing to be nervous about."

Nadia smiled. "Thank you. But I'll never be as good as her." She turned and looked up toward the stage.

I watched the band, all huddled together on the stage, laughing. They looked pretty relaxed, from what I could see. I turned to Nadia. "A few nights ago, before Gerard and I had our little run-in at the park, I saw him talking to Allen Brown. I'm sure you know who he is? The security guard at the town center?"

She nodded.

"I'm just curious... do you have any idea what Gerard would've been talking to him about?"

She shook her head and shrugged. "I don't know anything about it."

"But they *do* know each other?"

She looked around before she answered. "I... I guess so."

I said, "In fact, you played at The Tap one night, and Allen was there, watching you."

"He makes me nervous, the way he stares." She turned and looked toward the stage.

I said, "Did you ever mention that to anyone?"

Nadia shrugged. "Bonnie used to tell me he was harmless."

Before I could get another word in, she started toward the stage. "Gerard's here. I'd better get back up there." She walked away before I could get anything else out of her.

Gerard walked right up to me. "Mr. Private Detective," he said. "What are you doing here?" He turned and looked Alex up and down, smiling. "We could put you on stage, someone as beautiful as you." He gave her a nod. "You wouldn't even need to sing."

Alex rolled her eyes and looked away.

I said, "Hey, Gerard, maybe you can help me out..." I took a step closer to him. "I had an incident last night. I was jumped by three men. You know anything about that?"

Gerard stared back at me, clearly not in the least bit intimidated. "Why would I?" He shrugged. "I thought you and I were going to put our bad start behind us?" He pulled at his chin. "But I can't say I appreciate your accusations."

I said, "I'm not accusing anybody. I'm asking if you know anything about it. One of the men was about your size. He happened to be the one who hit me from behind, when I wasn't looking. You know how that works, don't you?"

"Perhaps your memory is foggy? I didn't hit you from behind." Gerard made a motion as if he was coming up to punch me with an uppercut, but moved his hand, as if in slow motion, and stopped, holding his fist under my chin. "It was just like that, wasn't it? Your eyes were right on me. You had to've seen it coming." Gerard grinned. "Was it because the man was perhaps a Latino, so you assume it was me—or someone I know—who gave you some trouble?" He looked toward the stage. "I didn't get the idea you were that type of person."

I stepped closer to him. "Don't play that bullshit with me," I said.

Gerard put his hands up, his palms out. "Take it easy, Mr. Private Detective." He stepped back.

I said, "Well, I just thought, since it was outside your buddy's apartment..."

"My buddy?"

I nodded. "Allen Brown."

"What makes you think he's my buddy?" Gerard turned to Alex and gave her a nod, pointing at me with his thumb. "You believe this guy?"

I wanted to wind up and knock him off his feet... show him his punch was nothing but a lucky one. But I knew better.

He walked away without saying another word, went around the outside of the stage and disappeared behind a curtain.

· · · · ● · ● · · · ·

When they started to play I was surprised by the sound. Although we'd heard Nadia and the band at the River Mist Café, the sound that came from the stage was different. It had a Pat Metheny sound. Or maybe a little Herbie Hancock.

Alex looked like she enjoyed it, her feet moving to the music.

Over toward the other side of the stage I spotted Amanda's friend Luis watching Nadia. He had two other men by his side.

A moment later he was approached by Gerard. The two appeared to get into a heated discussion, but then Gerard spoke into Luis's ear. Luis and the two thick, muscular men turned and looked out into the crowd.

I leaned into Alex to get her attention and pointed with my chin toward Luis.

She turned and yelled into my ear over the music. "Isn't that Luis?"

I nodded just as he turned and walked away from Gerard. And when he did, I noticed he seemed to have a limp to his step. The side of his face appeared to have a bruise.

I grabbed Alex by the hand as we worked our way through the crowd and farther away from the stage. There were more people now, the crowd still growing as Nadia and the band started to pick it up.

I tried to catch up with Luis. Although by the time we made it through the crowd he was nowhere to be found. I looked back toward the stage at Gerard. He'd had his eyes on me, and looked away as soon I made eye contact with him.

We made it to the parking lot. That's where we saw Luis as he stepped inside a gold Pontiac Trans Am. It was one of those older models, like the one Burt Reynolds drove in Smokey and the Bandit. But it was a different color. I didn't tell Alex that was my dream car as a kid.

I let go of her hand as I picked up the pace. I started to jog, then a full-out run as he seemed ready to leave. I cut across the lot at an angle and tried to cut off the Trans Am as it headed for the exit.

I don't know if he saw me or not, but the driver picked up speed as I approached.

I was now running as fast as I could to stop them.

But then my ears started to ring. The music seemed to fade into the background as the ringing in my ears grew louder.

My head started to ache and pound inside my skull. I felt like I was running fast but maybe I wasn't. My legs had started to feel numb.

I got closer to the Trans Am, now stuck behind a small crowd of people. A minivan backed out of a parking space and blocked the Trans Am from going anywhere.

A horn blew.

I cut around the van and yelled for Luis as I ran up along the side of the Trans Am.

The driver hit the gas, whipped the car around the van and headed for the exit. The tires smoked and squealed as the car hit the pavement on the street.

By the time I got to the end of the lot, the only thing I got was a whiff of burnt rubber.

I leaned over with my hands on my knees and tried to catch my breath. I saw stars. The ringing in my ears grew louder.

Alex came up behind me and put her hand on my back. "Are you okay?" she said.

I stood up straight and put my hands on my hips. But I couldn't answer her. I couldn't catch my breath. I could barely see.

"Henry?" she said. At least that's what it sounded like. Her voice echoed in my mind.

I saw not one, but two of her standing in front of me. I dropped to one knee... then fell to the ground. I looked up at Alex and saw her lips move. But I couldn't make out what she was saying.

I continued to struggle with each breath, the sounds around me muffled, until I closed my eyes and heard nothing else.

Chapter 26

ALEX WAS BEHIND THE wheel of my car when I opened my eyes.

"What are you doing?" I said, feeling pain in my throat as I spoke, my throat dry and soar.

She kept her eyes on the road. "I'm taking you to the ER." She gave me a quick glance. "You passed out."

I straightened myself up in the seat and wiped what might've been drool from my mouth. "What happened? Where'd Luis go?"

"You ran after Luis like a madman. But I didn't pay much attention to anything else once you passed out. I know he left in that Trans Am."

"He was at The Landing, right? I didn't dream that, did I?"

She seemed to force a smile and nodded.

I leaned my head against the back of the seat. The inside of my skull pounded. "Last thing I remember, we were running after Luis." I looked out the passenger window, up toward the city's skyline. "How long was I out?"

"Maybe ten minutes. You walked yourself to the car, for the most part."

I looked at her. "I don't remember."

She forced a smile. But I could see through it. I knew she was worried about me.

"I still say it's nothing," I said. "I know you think I'm ignoring it. Or that I'm not the least bit worried. I did Google it... could be stress?"

She turned and gave me a look. "I'm sure whatever you found in the search results is an accurate diagnosis. Might as well just head home."

I closed my eyes. "Whatever money we make on this case will end up going to the doctors. I hope you know that."

"Does that mean you're not going to fight me about going?"

I lifted my head from the headrest. "I'm not going to let them rack up a bill with thousands of dollars on it. But you know they'll try."

"Not every doctor is out to screw you," she said.

• • • • • • • • • • •

When we walked through the front door of the ER, the woman at the front desk remembered me right away.

"You're the investigator, right?" She narrowed her eyes. "You didn't get in another fight, did you?"

178

I gave Alex a look. I could tell she held back a smile.

I shook my head, turned to the woman behind the desk. "I passed out again." I leaned forward on the counter. "Passed out, short circuited... blacked out? I don't know what you call it, but my friend is convinced something's broken inside my head."

She looked up at me from behind the desk and smiled. "At least you walked in on your own two feet this time."

Alex stepped toward the desk. "He was running. And when he stopped... he fell to the ground."

"Running?" She looked up at me. "Exercising? Or were you—"

"I was chasing someone."

She kept her eyes on me for a moment.

My phone buzzed in my pocket. It was Billy.

"Where are you?" he said.

"I'm at the ER. Alex dragged me here to get my head checked."

"Uh oh. Did you pass out again?"

"I don't remember, to be honest."

The woman behind the desk stared at me, waiting.

I put my finger up to both of them. "I'll be right back." I walked out the front door and stood outside the building. I'd expected fresh air but the smell of cigarettes hit my face. I turned and saw two nurses sneaking a smoke around the corner of the building.

Billy said, "Have you seen the news?"

"No. Like I said, I'm at the ER."

"Don't they always have the news on?"

"I have no idea. Why?"

"You know that security guard you'd been following? The one from the town center?"

"Allen Brown?"

"Yeah, that's him. Well, they just found his body in the parking lot."

"Are you sure?"

"Yeah, I'm sure. I'm watching it right now."

I walked back inside with the phone still up to my ear. "What channel?"

"The ten o'clock news. But the weather just came on."

I held the phone away from my head and looked at Alex.

The woman behind the desk said, "Mr. Walsh, we really need to get you taken care of, would you please—"

I ignored her. "Alex, Billy's on the phone. Allen Brown is dead."

"How can he be dead?" She turned and looked toward the TV. It was a commercial.

"We must've just missed it." I put the phone back up to my ear. "Billy, did they say what happened?"

"I'm not sure," he said. "I looked up when they mentioned the St. Johns Town Center. I thought of you... but only caught the tail end of it."

We were both quiet for a moment.

Billy said, "Are you okay?"

I turned, looked at the woman behind the desk with her eyes on me. "I'll have to take a raincheck," I said.

I grabbed Alex by the hand and headed toward the door.

Alex pulled her hand free. "*Henry, you stop right now!* You can't leave. You have to at least *talk* to a doctor."

The woman behind the desk said, "She's right. You're crazy if you walk out that door."

I smiled. "I'd still be crazy one way or the other." I reached for Alex, grabbed her by the arm and pulled her out the door. "Come on, we'll come back tomorrow."

"Henry," she said.

But I ignored her and walked ahead toward the car. "Where'd we park?"

"*Henry!*" Alex snapped.

"Will you just tell me where you put my car?"

"We're on the other side." She stopped in front of me as I turned, put both of her hands on the sides of my face and looked me in the eye. It was dark, but it looked like she might've had tears. "You can't keep pushing yourself like this."

· · · ● · ● · · ·

We stopped in the town center's parking lot, right near the bridge within throwing distance of the courtyard and the River Mist Café. Most of the lot was closed-off with yellow police tape surrounding the scene.

There were dozens of people standing around in the parking lot, just outside the yellow tape. It was quieter than at any time I'd been there. The band that must've been on stage had stopped playing, although their instruments were still set up. The cymbals on the drum set reflected the blue lights from the Sheriff's vehicles.

Alex and I squeezed through the crowd just outside the tape. We worked our way close enough to see Allen's Crown Victoria with the missing police decals. We walked around so we could see straight toward the front of his car. The lights from above the parking lot reflected off the glass, making it almost impossible to see through the windshield.

But even with the reflecting light, the bullet hole in the glass on the driver's side was impossible to miss.

Alex nodded toward a small group of officers near the car. "There's Mike," she said. "Wait here." She ducked under the tape and walked toward Detective Stone.

Mike and I never got along very well, so I didn't resist when Alex told me to stay put. And when he turned to her, he looked my way.

I gave him a nod, but he turned away as if he hadn't noticed me.

I walked around the perimeter of the taped-off area and tried to get closer. I stopped where I could look inside the driver's side of Allen's car, and saw his body slumped forward, his head down against the steering wheel.

I looked around at the crowd and wondered if I'd recognize anyone. Gerard and Nadia, I assumed, were still at the Landing. Robert wouldn't be around this late, although I remembered I hadn't heard back from him. I wondered if that should worry me.

Alex walked back over and ducked under the yellow tape. "Just the one shot through the windshield," she said. "Got him right in the head. Said it was from a pretty good distance, from what it looks like so far."

I stared past her and watched Mike light up a cigarette as he laughed with a couple of officers. I thought it was disrespectful, although every cop reacted in their own way to a crime scene. I had a feeling Mike wanted to show the spectators he was relaxed, and that it wasn't his first rodeo.

Just another day on the job, folks.

I said, "So what else did he say?"

"Same thing he always says. He states the obvious." She crouched down and looked toward Allen in the driver's seat. "He might've told me more if I wasn't with you."

"Any witnesses?"

"You want to know what he said? He said to tell you he'd have a full report written up for you, and will make sure it's in your hands by morning." She gave me one of her looks. "He did say the car reeked of alcohol."

"Oh, now there's the big-time investigative work I was hoping for. "I turned and started to walk away.

"Are we leaving?"

I looked over my shoulder and nodded. "We're not going to get anywhere standing here."

Chapter 27

"THE COPS WILL BE here soon if we don't move fast," I said as Alex and I walked toward the patio off the back of Allen's apartment.

"Unless they're already inside," she said with a nod toward the sliding glass doors.

Lights bounced around inside as shadows moved behind the curtains.

We walked around to the side of the building to see if we could get a better look inside one of Allen's windows.

But there was a click... a distinctive sound I didn't have to hear twice to know what it was.

A man's voice from behind me and Alex said, "Don't either of you turn around, unless you want a piece of lead in your skull."

We both put our hands in the air as we faced the wall on the side of Allen's building. I tried to look over my shoulder, but felt the muzzle of the gun pressed into the back of my head.

"I told you. Don't turn around."

"Let's go," the man said with a hispanic accent as he grabbed the back of my shirt and shoved me toward the wooded area behind Allen's building. I was able to get a quick look at him, but his face was covered with a ski mask.

Up ahead through the woods were blue lights coming through the trees. The cops were on their way, likely right to Allen's apartment.

Whoever was behind us with the gun clearly didn't wait around to find out what was about to happen.

He ran straight past us and into the woods. I could barely see him, but could hear his quick feet as the leaves crunched and sticks snapped as he disappeared into the darkness.

A moment later two other men ran past us from Allen's apartment and disappeared behind the other man into the woods. They moved too fast and it was too dark for either of us to recognize them.

Alex said, "Maybe we should hit the road."

"Give me a minute," I said. "Cops come in, I'll catch up with you." I ran toward Allen's apartment.

"Catch up with me *where*?" she said, her voice raised but hushed.

I went inside the apartment through the sliding glass door without giving her an answer. The inside was a mess. The place was destroyed. I looked around for the computer but didn't see it. I knew it had either just been stolen, or Allen hid it somewhere. But I didn't have time to look for it. Not with the cops on their way.

I ran out the back, to where Alex was waiting for me. "Let's go," I said, and we ran through the woods until we made it out to the street, where I looked back and saw beams from flashlights bouncing around the exterior of the building and into the woods behind us.

We walked along the street, at the edge of the woods, trying to stay out of sight.

I heard a car's engine, quiet, almost like a low rumble or a purr, but I didn't see the car.

Alex grabbed me by the arm and pulled me into the woods, where we ducked behind a row of shrubs.

The card car was visible now, out on the street. But the lights were off. It was headed in our direction.

When it drove under a street light, I saw what it was. "It's the Trans Am," I said.

Alex said, "Is it Luis?"

I nodded, looking out from the woods. The gold Trans Am went slowly past us.

We both stood and watched the car. Once it got to the corner, the engine roared and the lights came on, tires squealing as the Trans Am disappeared into the night.

• • • • • • • • • •

Alex was behind the wheel when we drove away from Allen's apartment and what had turned into quite a commotion outside his building.

I looked down at my phone and read a text message from James:

The security guard from the town center is dead. Haven't been able to reach Amanda

I looked at Alex in the driver's seat. "You okay?" I said.

She nodded, her eyes still on the road.

As much as she'd been worried about me, I was just as worried about her. Alex hadn't slept much. Neither of us had, in fact. And I could see it in her eyes—even in darkness inside the car—she was tired.

"James sent a text about Allen. He saw it on the news. He tried to reach Amanda but couldn't."

Alex gave me a quick glance. "Like I said, we can't be so sure she's the innocent little sister."

I turned to her. "I don't think she was involved in Bonnie's death, if that's what you're trying to say?"

Alex didn't answer as she turned the wheel toward the ramp for Route 10. "No, I'm not saying that. But just because she's James's little sister doesn't mean she's free from guilt."

"We don't really know much about her," I said. "But she seems like a good kid. She's been through a lot." I looked at my phone. "I should call James."

She turned to me. "You need sleep. We both do. And just so you know, I'm still taking you to the doctor in the morning."

I called James and he answered on the first ring. "Henry?" he said. "Where've you been?"

"I saw your text. We were at the scene... Where Allen had been shot."

He said, "The news mentioned Bonnie, with this being the second death at the town center in less than a month."

I thought about that for a moment. "Your text said you haven't heard from Amanda?" I watched Alex. She seemed to enjoy the car's power.

"I've been calling her all night," James said. "When I heard about the shooting, I got worried. They didn't say who it was right away, so I had to make sure she was okay. But she hasn't answered my calls."

"I haven't seen her. But I did see Luis... at The Landing."

"You were there? Did you see Nadia?" he said. "I should've gone, but..."

"But a little weird around Gerard?"

James was quiet for a moment.

I glanced at Alex as she picked up speed. The Chevelle's engine roared. She seemed to enjoy the ride.

But when I looked at her face, I wasn't so sure.

"You okay?" I said, as I watched her from the passenger seat.

She glanced at me. Her knee bounced up and down. Her foot slapped the pedal against the floor. "*The brakes!*" she said. She turned to me with panic in her eyes. "They won't work... I can't slow down. *We have no brakes!*"

"James, I gotta go," I said without another word. I dropped the phone on the seat. I tried to sound calm. "Take your foot off the gas."

"What the hell do you think I'm doing?"

She gripped the steering wheel as if she wanted to peel the leather from the steel underneath. Her knuckles were white.

I took my seatbelt off and slid over. I got right up against Alex so we were both behind the wheel.

"What the hell are you doing?" she said.

I reached for the wheel and slid my foot down toward the brake pedal. But it didn't do a thing. "Switch seats," I said.

"Switch seats? *Are you crazy?*"

"Probably."

The car was already moving at a good clip. I glanced at the speedometer. It was close to seventy miles an hour. I tried to work my way underneath Alex as she climbed over me to the passenger side. Luckily I was able to keep the car on the road.

"We don't have much gas," I said. "We'll jump on the highway, drive until we run out of gas."

She yelled, "Are you serious? That's your plan?"

The steering wheel bounced in my hands. I had to raise my voice over the roar of the engine. "Do you have a better one?"

I hit the ramp for 95 from Route 10 at full speed. The Chevelle skidded sideways as we bounced and bottomed out. The undercarriage scraped against the road. We skidded sideways onto 95. I cut across two lanes into oncoming traffic.

I put my foot on the brake but there was nothing to it. The pedal was flat against the floor.

Brakes were not an option. And I knew the emergency brake didn't work, although it'd been on the list of repairs I still needed to make.

The accelerator was stuck and our speed continued to climb.

I tried to shift the transmission to a lower gear. But the engine screamed and the smell of burnt metal and rubber filled the inside of the car.

I worked the shift and hoped to get it into neutral, but it wouldn't budge.

We passed a sign: *CONSTRUCTION ZONE.*

Our speed climbed to eighty-miles-an-hour.

As loud as I could without screaming, I said, "*I'm getting on two-ninety-five. Hold on tight!*" I ripped the wheel for the exit and we skidded on the curve, made the corner and hit the Beltway at full speed.

In what felt like a handful of seconds, we blew past the North Main Street Exit. We passed the Pulaski Road exit.

But then we came around Zoo Parkway. That's when we saw the brake lights ahead.

Traffic was at a standstill.

A construction worker in an orange vest screamed and waved his arms and whipped his orange flags through the air. He dove out of the way as we crashed through the *LANE CLOSED* sign and blew past him doing eighty-five. We drove over dozens of cones as one after the other bounced up over the hood of the car.

I again tried to shift the transmission, but the stick still wouldn't budge. Even if I had tried to kill the ignition, I'd not only lose power steering but would've locked the steering wheel.

I spotted an opening in the guardrail up ahead. But I knew it'd be nearly impossible to cut the wheel at almost ninety degrees, doing over eighty-miles-an-hour, and make it through an opening no more than ten feet wide.

I had about four-seconds to decide.

I ripped the steering wheel toward the opening in the guardrail dividing the north and south lanes. The Chevelle fishtailed as I struggled to maintain control. The steering wheel shook violently in my hands.

Somehow, we made it through the opening. But as we drove through I clipped the corner of the guardrail with the rear-end of the car. It sent us into a tailspin as we slid across the highway on the northbound side.

I gripped the wheel and straightened the car as we somehow merged into oncoming traffic. I weaved in-and-out of traffic, passing cars on both left and right.

I looked down at the gas gauge. I yelled over the screaming engine. "*The needle's all the way down!*"

The car was on fumes.

In the rearview I saw blue lights coming toward us. The cops were close behind, as they surrounded us on all three sides.

We were in a high speed chase... as if I had a choice.

The cop to our left pulled ahead as the one on the right dropped back. The car just ahead of us nudged the front left side of the car and sent us out of control off the highway.

We drove over the grass and slammed down as we hit the lip off the highway.

We were headed straight for the trees.

I tried to maintain control until, finally, the engine sputtered. The speed slowed, as it dropped from eighty to sixty... To fifty...

The only thing straight ahead were trees. Too many to miss.

I turned the wheel to avoid the crash, but we bounced from the first tree we hit and the car spun around in the grass. We hit another tree with the back of the car and bounced off.

We were still moving too fast.

But I avoided another as we drove along the edge of the highway. I turned the wheel and took the car toward a long row of flowering shrubs.

It was just enough to slow us down and as the branches scraped along the side of my fresh-painted car... the engine finally died.

The gas gauge was well below *E*.

Officers jumped from their vehicles and surrounded us at gunpoint.

One of them screamed. "*Get out of the vehicle! Get down on the ground!*"

We did as they told us to, without question or argument. Down on our stomachs, we kept our hands on our heads.

I turned to Alex. "And the fun has only just begun." I tried to look up at the nearest officer. "I'm a private investigator. My reg is in my back pocket. My brakes didn't work. And the accelerator was stuck. "

One of the officer's reached for my wallet, took it out from my pocket and said, "So you're a private investigator. That doesn't mean you weren't driving reckless and out of control."

One of the officers reached inside and popped the hood. She leaned over the engine with her flashlight, fiddled around inside and came out, closing the hood. "This thing's been sabotaged."

The other officers tucked their guns in their holsters.

I said to Alex, "You okay?"

"I don't know," she said. "My heart's pounding like it's going to come out of my chest. But I'm happy to be alive."

A couple of the officers reached down and helped me and Alex to our feet. "Are you both okay?"

The officer with my wallet said, "Henry Walsh, huh?" He turned to the others. "This is the guy who helped Mike Stone solve Lance Moreau's murder."

Chapter 28

Two officers drove us back to Alex's house, and as we were almost there, the officer behind the wheel looked up at me in the rearview. "I don't know if anyone already asked you this or not, but where were you coming from before you realized you had no brakes?"

"Out visiting a friend," I said. "We were on our way back to Alex's house when the car started to act up."

His eyes shifted from the road to the rearview. "Where's this friend happen to live?"

Without hesitation, I said, "Just south of Arlington."

He looked at his partner in the passenger seat, then shifted his eyes back into the rearview. "You live out at Neptune Beach, right?"

I nodded, "Yes, sir."

"The reason I ask," the officer said, "is, well, that Chevelle you were driving is somewhat unique. Don't see many of 'em around anymore." He looked in the mirror, back at me again.

"I had a girlfriend with one in high school." He smiled as he looked up through the mirror. "Stuck with her a little longer than I would've liked, just so I could keep driving it."

I stared back at him and forced a smile, but wondered if he had a point.

"I heard something earlier tonight on the radio… about a car like your Chevelle spotted over at the Jax Atlantic Apartments, out Westside. Had a break-in of a man's home; a man who'd coincidentally been shot and killed earlier in the evening." He paused for a moment when dispatch came over the radio. He turned to the other officer in the passenger seat then back at me in the rearview. "Any chance you were over that way?"

The other officer turned in his seat and over his shoulder said, "Maybe snoopin' around over there?"

"Well, to be honest," I said, "we *were* driving by the area, saw all the police vehicles. We did stop to see what was happening. But we weren't there for more than four, five minutes."

The officer pulled his vehicle up into Alex's driveway.

I pulled on the handle before the car had even stopped, but when it wouldn't open I remembered I was in the back of a squad car.

The back doors, of course, don't open from the inside.

The officers both stepped out and opened both back doors so Alex and I could get out.

One said, "Did you see anything over there while you were snooping around?"

I shook my head. "We weren't snooping around. We just drove by. Like I said, we just stopped by when I saw a couple of Sheriff's vehicles with the lights on. I used to be a cop myself, so I can't help but be interested in—"

"You were a cop? Where?" he said.

"I was a Trooper up in Rhode Island. With the Rhode Island State Police."

"Rhode Island, huh? What brings you down here?"

"I'm *from* here," I said. "I had a good opportunity to go up there."

"How'd it work out? You retired?"

I shook my head. "You could say that."

· · · · ●· ● · · ·

Billy filled my coffee cup as he stood on the other side of the bar across from me and Alex. "So this girl's boyfriend... he's the one who painted the car?"

I shook my head. "No, it was his cousin."

Billy said, "I can't imagine it was just a coincidence."

My phone buzzed. It was James. "Give me a minute," I said to Alex and Billy as I got up from the bar and walked outside the restaurant. "James?"

"Henry? You hung up the phone last night and I didn't know what happened. I called you back but you didn't an-swer..."

"Yeah, I was cruising around with Alex."

He didn't say a word.

"What about Amanda, did she call you back?"

"Yes, she called this morning," he said. "I was worried all night. I hardly slept. Apparently she stayed with a friend."

"Do you know who?" I said.

"No, I didn't ask. She's a big girl. Although she does worry me a lot."

"Any chance she mentioned seeing Luis?"

"She didn't say."

I said, "I've seen him around quite a bit lately. Let's just say he seems to pop up in the wrong places."

"Is there something you want me to ask Amanda about him?"

"No, I'm going to talk to her myself. So don't mention we even talked about him. Do you know where she is?"

"She was on her way to work."

"At the carwash?"

"Yes. I wish she'd get a better job. I've tried to help, even offered to have her come work with me, but said she didn't trust people in real estate." He laughed.

"I gotta run, James. I'll catch up with you a little later." I hung up and went back inside and sat next to Alex at the bar.

She had her cup of tea in her hand, and her eyes down in her phone. When she looked up at me she said, "They're still questioning witnesses."

"I wonder if the Sheriff's Office will, off their presumption Bonnie's death was an accident. Allen's—clearly—was not."

Billy walked back over and stood in front of us on the other side of the bar. "Alex said you left the ER and haven't gone back to see the doctor?"

"Duty calls," I said.

"What about now? You're all right?"

"I seem to be." I knocked on the top of the bar with my knuckles.

"Maybe it's nothing," Billy said. "Stress can cause dizzy spells, could even cause you to pass out. I've seen it before."

"Now you sound just like him," Alex said to Billy. "He doesn't need convincing that passing out might be normal. Every time he tells me he's fine I end up having to pick him up off the ground with his eyes rolled back." She looked back and forth from me to Billy. "He can't just ignore this."

Billy said, "I didn't say he should ignore it."

She tapped on her phone and glanced at me. "I'm making an appointment. I don't care if I have to throw you in handcuffs to get you there." She got up from her seat and walked outside with her phone up against her ear.

I looked at Billy as I sipped my lukewarm coffee. "She's been acting weird lately. Like my mother."

Billy laughed. "You blame her? You think she wants to see something happen to you? She worries about you. What's wrong with that?"

• • • • ● • ● • • •

Alex drove her yellow Jeep into the car wash where Amanda worked. We parked and watched as Amanda leaned over the front of an older Lexus with gold rims and a thick chain around the license plate. With a towel in her hand, she leaned over and buffed the hood with circular motions.

The manager was inside his hut as I walked past him. He opened the window and said, "Buddy, you don't get off this property right now, I'm calling the cops."

I gave him a nod and smiled as I continued toward Amanda.

She straightened herself up off the hood when she saw me walking toward her.

"Henry?" She was surprised to see me. She stared back, her mouth hung slightly open as if she wasn't sure what to say.

I said, "Is everything okay?"

She shrugged. "Yes, I guess so."

"Mind if I ask where you were last night?"

She waited a moment before she answered and wiped her forehead with the back of her hand. "I was out with a friend." She didn't look me in the eye, but squinted with the sun shining down onto her face. "Why do you ask?"

"Well, for one, your brother was worried about you. He tried calling a few times, but you didn't answer. And, number two, I'm sure you heard there was another death at the town center?"

She nodded. "I heard."

"So where were you? What'd you do all night?"

She gave me a look. "I already have a big brother asking me too many questions I don't have to answer."

"I'm not asking you as a big brother," I said.

"I hope you don't think I had something to do with that security guard, do you?"

I shook my head. "I didn't say that." I looked around at the rest of the crew. "Where's Luis?"

"I don't know."

I kept my eyes on hers, but she looked off somewhere else. "Were you with him last night?"

"I haven't seen him."

"No? Are you sure? Because *I* did. And I get the feeling he was trying to get away from me."

She stared back at me. "What's that supposed to mean?"

"Nadia played at The Landing last night. I assume you knew that?"

Amanda nodded. "Of course. Is that where you saw Luis?"

"He drives a gold Trans Am, right?"

She waited a moment, looked toward her boss seated in the hut as he watched us. Amanda said, "I have to get back to work. I can't afford to lose this job. Last time you were here, he almost fired me."

"Sorry about that."

Under her breath, she said, "He's such a jerk."

"But, Amanda, you didn't answer me. Does the Trans Am belong to Luis?"

She shook her head. "Not that I know of."

GREGORY PAYETTE

"And you're sure you have no idea where he was last night?"

She crouched down on the ground next to the car and started to buff the door. With her back to me, she said, "I told you already, Luis is not my boyfriend. I don't track him everywhere he goes."

"Okay, well then what about Luis and Gerard? What can you tell me about those two? Maybe Luis does a little work for Gerard, on the side?"

She stood up and draped the towel over her shoulder. "Luis has helped Gerard out before. I don't know what... he doesn't tell me. And I don't ask."

"Does it have anything to do with the music business?"

Amanda turned to me and narrowed her eyes. "I told you, I don't know."

I turned to Alex as she waited in the Jeep. I put up a finger, let her know I'd be another minute. I said to Amanda, "I saw him get in the Trans Am at the Landing, then again right there at the town center, where Allen was killed."

She looked past me and bit her teeth down into her lower lip. "Okay, listen. I lied about not seeing him last night."

"Oh? Were you with him?"

"No. But I did see him. I was at the Landing, too. I only talked to Luis for a couple minutes. It was early. I hung back in the crowd... I didn't even want Nadia to know I was there." She swallowed hard. "Don't tell my brother."

"Were you lying when you said you didn't stay with him last night?"

202

Amanda shook her head. "No, that's the truth. I stayed at a friend's apartment."

I folded my arms at my chest, not sure if I could believe whatever came out of Amanda's mouth.

Chapter 29

Robert was out by the pond at the town center. He had a skimmer with a long pole in his hand and cleaned out the leaves or whatever else was floating at the surface of the water. There were a half dozen turtles out on a boulder in the middle of the pond, enjoying the late morning sun.

"Hi Robert," I said as I walked up behind him.

He seemed a bit startled and pulled the earbuds from his ears.

"Sorry," I said. "I didn't mean to scare you."

He pulled the skimmer in, dumped what he'd pulled from the pond into a plastic bag. He collapsed the pole down to half its size. "I guess you could say I'm a little jumpy, after what's happened." He looked down toward the ground for a moment and shook his head. "It's hard to believe. I don't know who would do such a thing to a man like Allen. It goes to show you what the world's coming to."

I said, "I tried calling you a few times a couple days ago. Did you take some time off?"

Robert nodded without looking my way. "I wasn't feeling well and spent some time in bed." I followed him as he walked away from the pond and around the building along to the courtyard. Walking a step ahead of me, he said, "When Allen took the job—about three, four years ago—I remember something he said. Along the lines of, 'as long as he didn't get shot he thought it'd be a pretty good gig, working security.'"

Robert and I walked around the corner to the side of the building. Robert stopped in front of a large steel door, reached into his pocket and pulled out a big ring of keys. He picked one from the bunch and slid it into the lock.

Inside was nothing more than a concrete storage room with tools and buckets and hoses. There was equipment on the floor, including a lawn mower and a power washer. He hung the skimmer on the wall then leaned down and grabbed a five-gallon, covered bucket from up against the wall and turned for the door. "Turtle feed," he said as he stepped out and locked the door behind him.

We walked back to the pond and I said, "Robert, did you ever see Allen have any trouble with anyone, outside of the ordinary?"

Robert put the bucket down on the concrete, removed the cover and reached his hand inside. He tossed the food into the water. "Now you're asking about Allen's death? What about Bonnie? You ever get anywhere with that?"

I turned and looked across the courtyard. The sign to the River Mist caught my eye. "The two may be related. But I don't know yet." I stepped closer to Robert and stood beside him as he tossed more food into the pond. "Robert, if you don't mind me asking... did you ever do any work over at Bonnie's house?"

He placed the cover back on the bucket. "A long time ago. I don't do it much anymore, but I'd take odd jobs here and there, whenever I could." He cracked half a smile. "It never hurts to have extra money. And when Bonnie asked if I could help..."

I put my foot up on the stone wall surrounding the pond. "The other day, when you saw me with Bonnie's husband... the way you reacted when you saw him just had me wondering if—"

"Her husband?"

I nodded. "James Chapman." I looked toward the table where James and I had sat. "I was over there having a coffee with him. When I saw you, you did an about-face when you looked at him. You disappeared, like you saw a ghost."

Robert shrugged. "I don't even know if I'd recognize the man. I remember seeing you, but I think you're maybe over-thinking things. I must've just been busy, and in the middle of something."

I looked toward the pond. "Is this the same time you normally come out to feed the turtles?"

He held up the bucket and nodded. "I feed them twice a day. Once around this time, then again before I leave. I try to mix in some vegetables, meat... I get scraps from the restaurants whenever I can."

"Is this what you were doing when you found Bonnie's body?"

He put the bucket down on the ground and looked off toward the sky. "Actually I'm late today. I try to do it a little earlier, around five or six... like that morning."

"But you didn't notice anything out of the ordinary that morning?"

He tilted his head. "We're talking about Bonnie now, correct?"

I nodded.

"I already told you—same thing I told the officers from the sheriff's office—I'd cleaned up some broken glass around the pond before I'd even..." He paused. "Before I saw her body."

I looked at him and waited a moment. "I don't recall you telling me anything about broken glass."

"No? Oh, I get confused with so many questions being asked. I must've confused you with the officer I spoke with. One of them—an officer in plain clothes—actually took the trash bag right out of the barrel." He pointed over toward a steel trash bin no more than ten feet from where we stood. "I told him I threw whatever I picked up right in there, never thought much of it at the time."

· • • • • • • • • ·

Alex had her hat down over her eyes and her feet up on the steering wheel as she waited in her Jeep for me.

"Are you awake?" I said as I stepped up into the passenger seat.

She sat up straight right away. Her hat fell off her head and down onto the ground.

"I'd be careful sleeping out here," I said. "Last guy known for taking naps in his car didn't make out so well." I walked around the other side of the Jeep and picked up her hat. "You think you can call Mike, see if he'd be willing to get us some information about the garbage bag someone pulled from the trash bin up there near the pond?"

"I'll try, see if he'll look into it." She turned the key in the ignition and started the Jeep. "Did I tell you about Doctor Francis?"

"*Who?*"

"Dr. Francis. The neurologist."

"No, I don't think so." I looked out toward the town center as she pulled out onto Town Center Parkway. "Give me his number and I'll call, make an appointment."

She gave me a look. "Oh, I'm sure you will." She paused, her eyes out on the road. "I already made an appointment." She glanced at me from the driver's seat. "So, what is it you're afraid of?"

"I'm not afraid. I'll go see him."

"Actually, the doctor's a woman."

"Okay, then I'm not afraid to go see *her*." I hesitated a moment and turned to Alex. "Okay, you want the truth? Maybe I'm afraid of what they might find. We've got a history of brain issues in my family, and..." I didn't finish

"So why is it, then, when you're working—or even when you're just having a casual conversation—you have to know every last detail. But when it comes to your own personal life—and your health—you stick your head deep down into the sand?"

I didn't answer.

Alex drove south on 295 and took the exit for 202. She said, "You worry about everyone else but yourself. That's why you're good at what you do—you put yourself last—but you can only do that for so long until you break. And if you don't have friends like me there to hound you..."

We were both quiet for most of the ride until Alex pulled up to the front of my apartment. She left the engine running. "Go get cleaned-up. I'll pick you up in two hours, take you to see Dr. Francis."

I sat still for a moment before I stepped out of the Jeep. "Will you at least call Mike, see what they might've pulled from that garbage bag?"

Alex nodded. "I told you, I'll try. But I'm sure he won't be able to make any promises."

She pulled away from the curb and drove off as I stood and watched until the Jeep turned the corner and disappeared.

I turned and walked toward the apartment. I still didn't feel comfortable with my surroundings. I wasn't sure I was happy with where I chose to live and, in fact, I felt like a stranger. It was the opposite of the years I spent at Trout River Marina, living on my boat.

Of course, the beach behind my apartment was great. Who wouldn't want that? The problem was, I rarely took the time to enjoy it or even sit out and look at the water.

I pulled out my wallet and looked at the phone number Earl'd given me at Billy's bar. I knew it was time to give his nephew a call and see if I could take a look at the boat he had for sale.

Chapter 30

I SPENT TWO HOURS with Dr. Francis and her team of brain people as they poked and prodded me and ran tests I wasn't sure I'd be able to pay for.

All I wanted was for someone to say I'd be fine so I could go back to normal... get behind the wheel without being worried I'd black out.

Alex looked up from the chair in the waiting room when I walked out of my exam. "Everything okay?"

I was surprised to see her. "You waited out here the whole time?"

"Almost."

I reached for the door and let Alex walk out ahead of me. "They don't know yet," I said. "The test results take a few days. Hopefully they'll know something soon." I gave her a look. "As long as they don't tell me I'm going to die."

"Well you *ARE* going to die," she said with a smile as she nudged me with her elbow. "Let's just hope it's not any time soon." We walked down the empty hallway toward the elevator. Alex turned to me. "It wasn't so bad, was it?"

I shook my head. "It was worth it, just to get you off my back. But if they do find something wrong, like they determine my small brain is simply rotting away. I hope you'll do the right thing and shoot me like a racehorse with a broken leg."

Alex rolled her eyes. She handed me a large, manilla envelope. "I met with Mike. A copy of the evidence log is in there, from the scene of Bonnie's death. He did say whatever we come up with, we can't tell anyone where we got it or try to use it as any kind of evidence."

I pulled the papers from the envelope. "So what if we find something we make sense of? Some proof?"

Alex said, "Mike'll deal with it then. For now, he doesn't want to know what we're up to."

We walked out of the building, across the parking lot and stepped into Alex's Jeep.

"Thanks," I said.

She had her body turned toward me, her arm up behind my seat as she backed out of the parking space. "As long as we keep in mind that anything Mike shares with us will need to be kept quiet. Word gets out... he'll be directing traffic, working a detail at the mall."

"Actually, I meant 'thanks' for taking me here... to see the doctor."

She turned the Jeep in the direction of the exit and stopped, put it in park and leaned over toward my seat. She reached out, put her arms around me and gave me a kiss on the cheek.

We stared at each other for a moment, our faces no more than six inches away from each other.

Alex let go of me and leaned back into her own seat. She looked in the mirror, straightened her hair, and put the Jeep in drive.

· · · · ● · ● · · ·

Luis sat in a chair out front of his cousin Renzo's auto body garage and looked toward me and Alex as we drove up the hill. Dust shot up into the air around us as dirt and stones kicked up from under the tires. Luis lifted his sunglasses and squinted, then got up from the chair and walked inside through the open garage door.

"Where's he going?" I said as I jumped from the Jeep before Alex had even stopped. "*Luis!*" I yelled. I turned to Alex and motioned with my hand. "Drive around back."

Alex spun the tires on the Jeep and took off around the corner, headed toward the back of the building.

I ran through the garage after Luis.

He went straight out the back door and down the hill behind the building.

Alex came sliding around the corner and slammed on her brakes in front of me. I grabbed the roll bar and jumped in the passenger side as Alex hit the gas and took off after Luis.

We bounced off our seats as she drove down the hill, the Jeep rocking back and forth through the rough terrain.

Luis ran fast through the tall grass as Alex did all she could to keep up with him while swerving to avoid the trees along the way.

She hit the gas as we'd caught up to him, driving alongside him as he ran as fast as his feet would take him.

I stood up from the seat with my hands extended and jumped for him. As I left the Jeep, my whole body in the air, Luis cut to the right, almost out of reach of my outstretched hands. But I grabbed a piece of his shit. He swung his fists behind him as I dragged him to the ground and we rolled together down the hill and stopped when we crashed into the base of a live oak.

Alex slammed on her brakes and the Jeep cut into the ground as dirt and dust kicked up from the tires. She jumped from her Jeep with her gun drawn and stood over Luis with her gun pointed toward him. "*Don't move!*"

The dust floated in the air around us as I got to my feet and brushed myself off. I looked down at Luis. "You might as well start talking." I glanced at Alex with the gun in her hand. "Luis, I have a feeling she's been dying to use her gun. She even told me there'd be a special bullet in the chamber for whoever destroyed my car and almost killed us."

214

Luis was still on the ground as he looked back and forth from me to Alex. His white shirt was covered in dirt and a spot of blood that came off his shoulder.

He tried to get up on his feet but I pushed him back down with my foot against his chest.

"I don't know nothin' about someone messing with your car. I didn't do nothin' to you. Why would I?" He tried to get up and I backed off as I let him get to his feet.

"If you run, Alex will put one in your leg," I said. "I guarantee it."

Luis bent down and picked his sunglasses up from the ground.

"So what were you doing at Allen's apartment? I saw you. I saw the Trans Am."

Luis stared back at me. He put his hand on the back of his neck as he looked down toward the ground. "I went to get something from Allen's apartment. That's all. I never expected to see you there... My friend outside... he didn't know who you were. Or else he wouldn't have pulled a gun on you."

"So who shot Allen?"

Luis's eyes widened as he shook his head. "Not me, man. No way, man. I ain't no murderer. I'm telling you, I was just supposed to go inside, grab a laptop and get out of there."

"The photos?" I said.

"Photos? No, man. Some music or something like that. I'm not really sure."

215

"So you want me to believe you didn't have anything to do with Allen being killed? But you were already in the apartment to grab his laptop while his body was still warm?"

"Honest in God, man. I'm telling you the truth."

"Is that why you were talking to Gerard at Nadia's show?"

Luis looked off for a moment, up toward the steel building.

"You took off as soon as you saw me," I said.

"Nah, man. I didn't mean nothin' by that. Just needed to be somewhere, that's all. I was already late." He shrugged. "No time to chat. You know what I'm sayin'?"

"Running late for what, to shoot Allen?" I gave Luis a nod. "Is Gerard the one who hired you to do it?"

Luis shook his head. "I didn't do it. How many times you gonna ask me the same question? All I was supposed to do was get that computer."

"Okay, but is Gerard the one who told you what to do?"

Luis narrowed his eyes. "He didn't tell me what to do, like I'm his *bitch*. He paid me... paid me to do a job."

"What's the difference?"

"Between what?"

"He told you to do something. You said he didn't tell you, but he paid you. I'm confused," I said.

Luis stared back at me, maybe at a loss for words.

I said, "Is your cousin up there?"

Luis shook his head. "You got a problem with the work he done?"

216

I stared back at him and took a step closer. "Either you're really good at playing dumb, or..."

Luis started walking back toward his cousin Renzo's shop. "He ain't there now. But I'll tell him, give you a call." He stopped and turned toward me and Alex. "I can tell you one thing for sure... Renzo don't know nothin' about the inside of a car. He's a body man, nothin' else."

Chapter 31

I RECOGNIZED A HANDFUL of the faces seated at the bar at The Tap, even though I'd only been there the one time I'd gone looking for Allen.

Alex and I grabbed a couple of stools at the bar.

I gave the bartender a nod. "Hey Brianna, remember me?"

She nodded. "Of course. Yes, you were here for Allen." She wiped the space on the bar in front of us. "Harry, right?"

"Well, you can call me Harry if you'd like." I tipped my head toward Alex. "This is Alex." I looked around for a moment and said to Brianna. "It's Henry."

"Oh... right. Henry. I'm so sorry."

"I've been called worse," I said.

Brianna had a smile for a moment, but it dropped from her face. "Jack Daniels?"

I nodded once. "Now that you ask..."

She turned to Alex. "Can I get you a drink?"

But I could feel Alex looking at me. I knew she wanted to tell me I should lay off the whiskey.

"Get her a shot of Jack," I said. "She needs it." I smiled as I glanced at her. "Relax, will you?"

Alex stared back at me for a moment, looked back at Brianna. "I'll have a bottle of beer. Budweiser's fine"

Brianna poured Jack into a glass and dropped two cubes inside. She grabbed a beer for Alex and gave us our drinks. She leaned with her hands on the bar. "All these years Allen had been coming here, nobody really got to know him. I remember, back when he first started coming in, he used to have his camera with him. He used to talk about all the songs he'd write. He was so creative. But then he just stopped. Anyone asked about his music, he wouldn't even talk about it."

"Any idea what happened?" I said. "And why he might've stopped?"

Brianna took a moment before she answered. "I'm sure it was because of his wife."

"His wife?" From the corner of my eye I caught one of the men staring at me from down the other end of the bar. He looked away when I turned to him. "Allen was married?"

Brianna nodded, walked down the other end of the bar and poured a couple of drinks for two customers who'd just walked in. She came back our way. "He used to come in with her once in a while. Didn't spend every day at the bar back then like he had the past few years."

"What happened to her?"

"She got sick. Took everyone by surprise." Brianna snapped her fingers. "Like that, she was gone." She looked over her shoulder toward the kitchen window, then leaned with her elbows down on the bar, her hands folded in front of her between me and Alex. She looked back and forth. "When I heard he was dead, the first thought I had was he'd killed himself."

Alex and I looked at each other as Brianna straightened up off the bar.

"Because of his wife?" Alex said.

"He was never the same after she died."

I looked up at the framed photos on the wall, mostly black and whites. "You said the other day he took some of these photos?"

She turned and nodded. She pointed to one of Ray Charles and another man. "This is Marty—the owner—with Ray Charles." She looked back at me and Alex. "He lived in Jax as a teenager."

I nodded as I stared at the photos.

"Allen told me once, a while ago, how he liked taking pictures when he wasn't writing because it let him use a different part of his brain. He said he didn't have to think as much when he took photos." She smiled. "I always thought that was interesting."

I didn't tell her about the photos I'd found on his laptop or even that I'd found the songs.

Brianna said, "The only time I overheard him talking about his music—and this wasn't that long ago—was when he mentioned Bonnie liked what he wrote. He looked pretty happy when he told me that... for the first time in a while."

· · · ● · ● · ● · ·

Alex and I were back at my apartment. We sat outside on the balcony on two wooden chairs.

Alex said, "You've been here, what, five or six months? And you won't even get decent chairs... with such a beautiful view to enjoy?"

I sat straight and tried to get comfortable, but it wasn't easy. I slid the chair closer to the railing and put my feet up on top. "I called about that boat Earl's nephew wants to get rid of."

Alex slid her chair closer to the railing and put her feet up on top. "You won't mind giving up this view?"

I turned to her. "You know what? I walk past my neighbors here. They barely say hello. I mean, the view is nice. But there's more to it. The truth is, after a while it's like staring at the same picture every day. You might think I'm nuts, but it's already gotten a bit old."

"And you think living on a boat is better?"

"It's just different. Maybe I like the motion. Maybe it's something about being grounded." I had my eyes out toward the ocean.

"I think you prefer to be the floating boat... *not* wanting to be grounded." I could feel her stare at me, but I kept my eyes on the ocean.

Alex's phone rang. She looked at the screen and put it up to her ear. "Sorry," she said. "Hello?" She was quiet for a couple of moments. She turned and looked at me as she listened to whoever was on the other end. "That's interesting." She waited a moment. "Anything else?" She was quiet again. "Okay, I really appreciate it. I owe you one." Quiet. "Uh huh, you bet. I owe you."

She hung up. "That was my friend from the lab. I called her to see if she could look at the glass they pulled from that trash bag at the town center... I hadn't heard back from Mike yet, so I gave her a call."

"What'd she say?"

"They were able to determine the glass that'd been swept up at the scene had dairy residue and traces of alcohol. She wasn't the one who'd examined it, but she said the glass isn't something they'd serve ice cream in. It was a bar glass."

"Alcohol?"

"Yes."

"Did she say anything about Codeine?"

Alex shook her head. "No."

Chapter 32

I WENT OUT TO see James at his house but didn't call ahead of time. He'd said he had a lot going on with work and might be hard to reach. It seemed he was always busy, more worried about his real estate business than whatever else was going on around him until, perhaps, it was too late.

He appeared surprised when I showed up at his door. He wore a white, terrycloth robe and held a cup of coffee in his hand.

"Henry? I didn't know you were coming over." He pulled the door half-closed behind him as he stepped outside but held onto the knob behind his back. "I don't have time to talk right now. I'm working on a pitch for a big listing... a beautiful home in San Marco." He forced a smile, but something was off.

"Can I come in?" I stepped through the door past him without waiting for an answer.

"Henry, you can't just—"

As soon as I was through the doorway I looked toward the kitchen and Nadia stood in bare feet with wet hair. She wore a matching, white robe.

"Oh, uh…" I turned to James and pointed with my thumb toward Nadia. "Is she your client?"

"It's not what it looks like. She's just… she needed a place to stay."

Nadia said, "Gerard and I had a fight."

"Henry," James said as he stayed near the door, his hand still on the knob. "Now's just not a good time. I really do have to get to work."

"I'll get out of your hair in a moment." I looked back and forth from James to Nadia. "But first, I'd like one of you to tell me what you know about Allen Brown?"

"You think he killed Bonnie?" James said.

"I don't know. But that's not what I'm asking. I want to know more about her relationship with him."

Nadia's eyes opened wide. "Bonnie would never be involved with a man like him."

I shook my head. "That's not what I mean. Although I can't say for sure what his feelings were toward *her*. But, James, I believe after she looked at those songs he sent her, she might've shown him some interest. Apparently, there was more to him… he wasn't just a strange man who worked as a security guard."

"What does this have to do with Bonnie's death, if you don't think he killed her?"

"I don't know if he did or didn't. But if Bonnie *was* trying to help Allen, maybe she stepped on someone else's toes." I turned to Nadia. "What if Gerard knew of Allen's talent as a writer? What if he'd decided he didn't want Bonnie to have them to herself?" I looked back and forth from James to Nadia. I looked Nadia in the eye. "What if he wanted them for you?"

· · · · ● · ● · · ·

I parked Alex's Jeep a block away from Gerard's apartment, cut through the playground and up the hill around the back of his building. I tried to stay out of sight, because I had a feeling Gerard might've had people watching out for him.

I knocked on his door and waited. I didn't want to knock too hard and draw attention from the neighbors. But before I tried to get inside his apartment, I needed to be sure the place was empty. I knocked again, then backed away from his door. I looked up and down the hall. There didn't seem to be anybody around.

My dad owned a watch repair business in Fernandina Beach. But there was a time when things got slow and he expanded into the locksmith business. So when I was a kid, I learned how to pick a lock. And the set I had in my pocket was the one he used when he'd first started the business.

I opened the lock-pick case, pulled out the right pick and stuck it in the doorknob.

It was a piece of cake with the construction-grade locks builders put on the same cookie-cutter apartments.

I had the knob turned in thirty-seconds, then stuck the pick inside the bolt-lock just above the knob. That one was a little more of a challenge, but within a little less than two minutes I had the door open.

I looked behind me, pushed open the door and stepped inside Gerard's apartment.

There was a nasty smell inside, a mix of scented soap and cheap men's cologne.

I walked down the hall and looked in a room with an un-made bed. There was a bathroom off the room, with the light inside still on. The mirror was still covered in steam. And I wondered if Gerard was hiding.

I looked under the bed and inside the closets. He wasn't there. Although, by the looks of it, I'd just missed him.

I looked down between the edge of a couch and the wall and found Allen's laptop, right there on the floor. I picked it up, removed the plug and put it up on the kitchen counter. I lifted the cover and searched the folders where Allen had the photographs stored. The other folder had the songs Allen had allegedly written.

As I was about to double-click one of the folders, something on his desktop caught my eye. It was a document with Gerard's name on it. I clicked it open and skimmed over the first page.

It was a contract between Gerard and Allen. I clicked through the pages and read a paragraph that spelled out what was going on: Gerard had bought—or was about to buy—the rights to Allen's songs.

I pulled out the thumb drive Alex had given me to copy the files. I stuck it into the USB port on the side of the laptop and dragged the contract to my portable memory stick.

I then dragged the folder with Allen's songs to the thumb drive.

I opened the photograph folders. There were dozens of folders within folders within folders. He looked to have them fairly well organized.

I opened some of the images while I waited for the files to finish copying. Some were of Bonnie posing for the camera, some of her performing on stage. There were photographs of Bonnie with other people in the photo, including the band.

There was a closeup of Bonnie and Amanda making a toast with their glasses raised in the air in front of them.

I turned toward the door when I heard something—or someone— outside the apartment.

I closed the photos and dragged the folders to the memory stick. I heard a voice outside. The files copied over but not as fast as I would've liked.

I looked across the apartment toward the balcony beyond the sliding glass doors. The layout in the place wasn't much different than what I had in my own apartment. Or, really, any apartment I'd ever been in like they were all constructed by the same exact builder.

I watched the progress of the photos being copied. "Come on," I said under my breath, as if that would speed it up. But the files copied were only at forty percent. It was taking too long.

There was a knock. I turned...

A voice came from the other side of the door. "Gerard? Please let me in, baby. I want to talk to you. I'm sorry... I don't have my key. Please let me in."

It was Nadia. I again looked back toward the balcony. If Nadia didn't have her keys, maybe I had nothing to worry about. I had time...

I looked down at the laptop. The files were eighty-percent copied... almost there. Ninety percent...

But then it stopped. The progress bar that showed me how many files were copied seemed to freeze.

I didn't know what to do. I couldn't take the chance of losing everything if nothing had actually copied over. If I removed the thumb drive from the laptop I could end up with nothing at all.

I wasn't sure Nadia was still outside the door. But I heard the knob wiggle. Whoever was outside slipped a key in the door.

I closed the laptop's cover, tucked it up under my arm and ran across the room. I opened the sliding glass door and made it out to the balcony.

The door to the apartment opened as I climbed over the railing and stood on the edge of the balcony. I tucked the laptop into the back of my pants and used both hands to grip the railing.

I crouched down, turned and faced the railing, and held onto the steel balusters as I let my feet hang down toward the ground. But as I let go and started to drop, the computer slipped from my pants. My feet hit the ground at the same time the laptop smashed on the concrete below me.

Chapter 33

I SAT AT THE table in Alex's kitchen and stared at the broken pieces of the laptop that smashed when I jumped from the balcony off of Gerard's apartment.

Alex turned the corner and sat next to me with her laptop out in front of her. She ran a cable from what was left of Allen's laptop and plugged it into hers.

I slid the memory stick toward her. "I'm pretty sure what we need is on here."

She took the memory stick in her hand. "We'll find out." She tapped the keys on her laptop.

"Gerard's going to know it was me," I said.

Alex kept her head down on the laptop. "Why's that?"

I shrugged. "He'll just know. Not that it makes much of a difference. But he knows I know he's hiding something. And whatever it is that's on here... he'll have no choice but to come clean."

Alex gave me a look. "Or he'll try to take you down before you figure it out on your own."

I got up and watched over her shoulder and pointed to the screen as one folder after another started to show up on the laptop. "There were hundreds of photos. Thousands." The document with the contract I'd looked at earlier showed up on the screen. I pointed. "Can you print that?"

Alex clicked a couple of keys and stood up from her chair. She walked to the other room, came back a moment later and handed me the pages. "What is it?"

I flipped through the pieces of paper. "It's a contract of some sort. Gerard's name is at the bottom."

I handed it to her and she scanned over the document. "This is a rights agreement. Gerard was going to buy the rights to Allen's songs."

"Where do you see that?"

Alex leaned over and pointed to the page. "Right here. This paragraph, halfway down. It spells it out. He was going to pay Allen for the songs he wrote."

My eyes focused on what looked like a list of songs on the back of one of the sheets of paper. I recognized some of them. "What's this?" I pointed to the page. "Five thousand dollars? What's that for?"

Alex looked down at Allen's broken laptop. "If this was still in one piece, I might be able to get to his email, see what kind of communication he had with Gerard... assuming he emailed this document to him."

"Five thousand dollars isn't much money," I said.

"It is for someone down on his luck."

I nodded. "Gerard probably convinced Allen it was a good deal. So then Allen sells the rights to him."

Alex flipped through the pages. "Is there anything about long-term payments? Maybe Allen would've gotten a cut of whatever profits came out of it?"

I thought for a moment. "What if Allen realized this deal was a bad one, and he decided not to sign it?"

Alex looked up from the paper. "What if Bonnie was trying to help Allen, and she was the one who told him it was a bad idea? That wouldn't go over too well with Gerard."

"And, of course, he blames Bonnie for ruining what could've been a lucrative agreement."

· · · ● · ● · · ·

Alex and I spent the next two hours going through the photos we'd copied from Allen's laptop. We printed out just about every photo that might've helped us make some kind of connection.

"Don't you find some of these a bit creepy?" Alex said. "If this isn't the definition of a stalker, I don't know what is. Hundreds of these are of Bonnie."

"At least," I said. I turned the laptop toward Alex and got up from the chair to stretch my back. I crouched down and pet Alex's dog, Raz.

"Nadia's always in the background when they're on stage," Alex said. She held a photo out for me she'd just printed. "Look at the way she looks at Bonnie from behind."

I said, "She was nothing more than a backup singer back then. She doesn't even play an instrument... she just sings."

I sat back down next to Alex and flipped through some of the other photos Alex'd printed. Another photo caught my eye. "Look at this one, of Amanda." I turned the photo so Alex could see it. "She looks mad, doesn't she?"

"Could just be resting-bitch-face," Alex said.

"Is that really a thing?"

Alex looked at more photos on the computer. "Although here's another one... Amanda has the same look on her face. She's shooting daggers at Bonnie, isn't she?" She turned the laptop so I could see it.

I looked in closer. "What's that in her glass?" It looked like chocolate milk. I thought about Nadia and her White Russians.

Alex shrugged. "No Idea. But she's got that look on her face again. She's clearly upset about *something*."

I looked at the photo in Alex's hand. "Look at Luis. He's practically on top of Bonnie, and she doesn't seem to mind."

Alex turned and looked up at me. "But I'd say Amanda does... with that look on her face." She stopped and held up another photo. "Look at this one. Looks like Bonnie and Amanda are having some kind of argument, don't you think?"

I nodded and leaned in closer. "And neither knew Allen was taking their picture."

Chapter 34

Nadia was seated at the bar at the River Mist Café with a couple of members of her band I'd recognized.

I walked up behind her and asked her what she was drinking.

She turned and looked at me over her shoulder, not looking the least bit surprised to see me. "A White Russian." She smiled with a shrug. "What else?"

"You mind if we have a few words," I looked at the men from her band, three of them with their eyes on me. I said to her, "Can we step outside?"

She picked up her drink and walked toward the door. I followed her outside where she sat at the table with the open umbrella. She looked up at me as I pulled out a chair. "No drink for you tonight?"

I shook my head and looked down at her glass. "So about this *thing* you have going on with James..."

"Thing?" she said as she turned the straw in her drink. She looked down into her glass. "I know how it looks. But James and I..." She shrugged. "It's nothing. Bonnie was my friend. I would never—"

"Do anything to hurt her?" I said, before she could finish.

She looked me in the eye and shook her head. "No, I would never have hurt Bonnie. How could you even think I would? She did so much for me. She helped me grow as a singer. To think someone would accuse me of hurting her?" She picked up her drink and took a sip.

"You like being out front now, though. No more in the background... where you get little respect."

Nadia narrowed her eyes. "This is my dream. I have a long way to go, but all I ever wanted to do—since I was a little girl—was perform and make people happy."

"But singing backup wasn't part of the dream, was it?"

She looked at me but didn't say a word.

I said, "Maybe once you had your own songs, you thought everything would change for you. Is that why Gerard had to get his hands on what Allen wrote? He'd pay him just enough money to shut him up, pay for his booze for a few weeks. That puts you at the front of the stage, a new level in your career with songs Bonnie knew were special. Maybe Gerard would even tell people you wrote them yourself?" I leaned toward her over the table. "But Bonnie knew you couldn't write your own music, and you were afraid she—"

"You are wrong!" Nadia yelled, then closed her eyes and seemed to take a deep breath. "Henry, I did nothing like that." She put her hand over mine. "Bonnie is the one who told me

Allen could help me, that he had talent... that it made sense for us to work together."

I pulled my hand back and stared into Nadia's eyes. "I'm sorry, Nadia. But I don't believe you. I don't believe you cared about Bonnie the way you say you did. I'm afraid you were jealous. Jealous of her talents... jealous—for some reason—of her husband."

She looked past me. Her eyes moved toward the turtle pond at the far end of the courtyard. "Bonnie didn't need Allen. She wrote her own music. She could sing, she could write... she played every instrument." She looked back at me with tears in her eyes. "She didn't want this anymore. She grew tired of it all. I remember when she told me she was walking away... she said her time had passed."

"So what about Allen? What about his songs?"

She looked down into her drink. "Bonnie wanted to make sure Allen would be paid enough for his talents. But Gerard wanted to play hardball. Allen almost did it... he almost signed the rights over to Gerard for, I don't know how much, around—"

"Five thousand dollars," I said.

Nadia raised her eyebrows. "Oh, it sounds like a lot, but... I don't know. Like I said, I didn't get involved. But Bonnie tried to help. She's the one who stepped in and stopped Allen from making a mistake."

"Must've got you and Gerard pretty upset," I said.

"Of course, Gerard wasn't happy. But I believe he knew Bonnie was right. After Bonnie died, Gerard promised Allen he'd make him a better deal. So they were talking, trying to find something that worked for all of us." She cracked a crooked smile. "It's not like Gerard has a lot of money himself, you know."

"But then, coincidentally, Allen's found dead." I turned and looked toward the parking lot where it'd happened. "Right here, in the middle of suburbia." I looked into Nadia's eyes. "You expect me to believe it was all just a coincidence?"

Nadia shook her head. "If you think I know what happened to Allen, I don't. Gerard's not perfect. He's not even a good boyfriend. But I do not believe he is a murderer."

I sat quiet for a moment, my eyes on Nadia. "Where is he now?"

"Gerard?"

"Yes."

"He drove down to Miami for a meeting with a record producer."

"Yeah? I bet he thought he'd have Allen's songs with him... the ones he took when he stole Allen's laptop the night he was killed."

Nadia's eyes opened wide. "How do you know he did that?"

"Because I took it back from him... right out of his apartment."

• • • • • • • • • •

Alex and I sat out back of James's house. He brought us out a plate of fruit and muffins and bagels. And, again, the fresh pitcher of juice I wondered if he squeezed himself.

He went back inside and came out with a dark, wooden box and put it down in front of Alex. "Now that I know you like tea..." He opened the top. "Take your pick." He poured her a cup of hot water.

"James," I said. "You have to tell me the truth about you and Nadia."

"The truth? I already told you I—"

"You said you messed around with her. But she didn't say a word about it. She said nothing ever happened."

James broke off a piece of bagel, spread cream cheese on top and popped it in his mouth. As he chewed he said, "We're just friends. That's the truth."

"There's really nothing else there? Because if she's in love with you..." I thought for a moment. "Let's be honest. You kept whatever happened between the two of you a secret from me. And I really wished you hadn't. It just makes me think, perhaps, Nadia is the one who might've wanted Bonnie dead the most."

James seemed to almost choke on his bagel. He held the cloth napkin up in front of his mouth as he coughed. He took a drink and said, "Nadia did *not* kill Bonnie. I would bet my life on it."

I took a sip of coffee. "Even though Bonnie had everything Nadia wanted?" I held my cup in front of my mouth, and said. "And that includes *you*."

James brushed his hand through the air toward me. "She doesn't want me at all. Sure, some things happened between us that probably shouldn't have. But they were purely physical. She's even said once or twice... that I'm more like her big brother." His plastic smile was back on his face.

I squirmed in my seat and glanced at Alex... her eyes opened wide.

"Bonnie was a good person," James said. "She took care of everyone. Especially her friends."

"I understand that. But you also told me you thought she was cheating on you. Did you forget about that?"

James crossed one leg over the other, looked down at his hands resting on his knee. "I don't believe she was faithful. But maybe part of that was my fault. I wasn't there for her. She was still a beautiful person."

I leaned on the table and looked him in the eye. "You've yet to even provide a *clue* as to who you believe she might've been fooling around with. Yet you're certain she was cheating."

James was quiet for a moment. He took a deep breath. "I'm going to ask you not to repeat this. I... I realize you may need to use whatever information I share with you, but this will hurt someone close to me if it gets out."

"Are you going to tell me you know who it was?"

James waited a moment. He closed his eyes and nodded as he looked down toward the table. When he looked up, he said, "Luis."

"Wait," I said. "Do you mean... Bonnie and Luis?"

James slowly nodded his head. "He denied it, of course. He told me he was helping her around the house."

"Helping her around the house? You mean, he was, how should we put this... acting in lieu of, say, a pool boy?"

James looked down at his hands resting in his lap. "I came home one day. Bonnie wasn't expecting me. I had a showing that day, but it was canceled. So I walked in the front door and," James took a breath. "Luis ran out the back door."

Alex and I exchanged a look.

James looked past us. "Bonnie said nothing had happened. There was nothing going on. He just left out the back door in a hurry, but she couldn't even come up with what he was doing there. She wasn't a very good liar... because most of the time she told the truth. But I knew what'd happened. I just knew."

Alex said, "Was Amanda with Luis at the time?"

"No, she didn't know him then. In fact, it was Bonnie who introduced them. She had still denied anything happened... and I always felt she tried to get Luis and Amanda together to cover it up."

"But Amanda and Luis never got together?"

He nodded. "At first, yes. But he broke it off... told her they should just be friends. I have a feeling it was because of Bonnie. And I wonder if Amanda—at some point—figured it out."

Alex said, "So Amanda knew about Bonnie and Luis?"

James didn't answer right away.

He sipped his orange juice. "I don't know. They were close—Bonnie did a lot for Amanda—but something was wrong."

"Wrong?" I said. "In what way?"

"Amanda said she wasn't sure I should trust Bonnie."

"She must've known," I said.

James shrugged. "I don't know." He leaned back in his chair, ran his hand through his hair. "I remember when Amanda had an accident. It wasn't that long ago. And Bonnie tried to help her, but she told Bonnie she didn't want her help."

"A car accident?"

James shook his head. "She was working on a car for a friend. Something slipped."

"What do you mean, 'she was working on a car?' "

"She was underneath it and I guess the jack slipped. Almost crushed her..."

Alex said, "I had no idea she knew anything about cars, other than how to wash them."

James nodded. "Amanda? You bet. She could pull an engine apart and put it back together. Ever since she was a little girl... she'd hang out at my uncle's auto repair shop."

Chapter 35

AMANDA SAT ON A picnic table under the live oak up on the hill just outside the metal building where Luis's cousin Renzo had his auto body shop.

The sun beat down on the dry soil, with dust coming up from my feet as I walked toward her.

She took a drag of her cigarette and stood from the picnic table as I approached. She stared back at me, but didn't say a word.

"How come you never told me you were a mechanic?" I said, from across the picnic table between us.

She crushed her cigarette out in a seashell on top of the table. With her eyes right on me, she shrugged one shoulder and said, "What's it matter? I know a little."

"That's not what James said. I hear you can take an engine apart, put it back together. Something you learned working with your uncle."

She looked down towards the ground. "My father died when we were young. Not that he was around much before then anyway. My uncle—my mother's brother—used to let me hang around his shop." She turned, looked toward the blue, metal building behind us. "It was something like Renzo's place. But not in the middle of nowhere, like this."

I folded my arms at my chest and put my leg up on the picnic table's bench. "I hear you hurt your back?"

"It's okay. Working at that car wash doesn't help, either."

I glanced behind me toward Alex, waiting in her Jeep. I looked Amanda in the eye. "I assume you expected me to be dead?"

She chewed on the inside of her lip and looked in her pack of cigarettes, but it was empty. She crushed the pack in her hand and tossed it on the picnic table. She stared back at me for a moment, her eyes squinted in the hot, bright sun. She didn't say a word.

"You must've been surprised," I said. "When you heard I was alive." I smiled. "No brakes, jammed accelerator... still not sure how we walked away from it."

Amanda looked behind her toward the tree. She looked up into the branches then over toward the blue, metal building. She swallowed hard and looked me in the eye. "I guess I knew you'd eventually figure it out. You're smarter than the cops."

"There was White Russian on the broken glass Robert had cleaned up the morning before he found Bonnie. I was sure it was Nadia. But you were the one who turned her onto them.

I never even saw you drink. Mostly soda. But when I saw your frosty drinks in the photos, I realized it was your favorite drink. And a few of the bartenders around the area confirmed that."

She closed her eyes for a moment. "It was an accident, you know."

"An accident? Was it an accident that you slipped codeine in her drink, too?"

"No, I didn't slip anything into her drink. Bonnie took care of that herself. I might've been the only one who knew she was addicted to painkillers. That was her own doing. She'd only have a few drinks and she'd be out of control." Amanda stared back at me. "I swear, Henry... I didn't mean to kill her."

"But you knew how drunk she was? And for some reason you still went after her and backed her into that rope?"

Amanda shook her head. "No, you have it all wrong. We weren't getting along at all. Our relationship had gone downhill long ago... and that night, it all came to a point... things just erupted."

"So you killed her?"

"No! She pushed me. She even swung at me. I'm telling you, she lost her mind. She'd started to push everybody away that loved her. Including James. And when I confronted her about cheating on him, she said she'd kill me if I told James."

"So you knew she slept with Luis, correct?"

Amanda nodded. "But she denied it. And so did Luis."

"Is that why you killed her? Because she slept with the man you were in love with?"

245

Amanda shook her head. "*Stop saying that!* I didn't kill her. It was an accident. I swear. She pushed me. I started to walk away from her and she grabbed me. Like I said, she took a swing at me. That's when she knocked my drink from my hand. Then she told me Luis loved me."

"So how'd she end up in the water?"

"All I tried to do was protect myself. When she swung at me, I... I pushed her back. That's all I did. But she fell over the rope and hit her head on the edge... went right down in the water."

"You didn't try to save her?"

Amanda shook her head. "I panicked. I'd been drinking, too. And I was afraid someone saw us arguing earlier."

"Allen?"

She nodded. "He was always watching her." She started to shake. Tears came down her face.

"Amanda, you know James will do whatever he can to help you. He loves you."

She sat on the seat of the picnic table and looked up at me, tears coming down her cheeks. "He knows?"

I shook my head. "Not everything." I turned, gave Alex a nod with my chin.

I turned back to Amanda. "Did you know I dated Bonnie in high school?"

She made a face. "Really? What happened?"

I gave it a moment. "She cheated on me."

· · · · ● · ● · · · ·

246

Two cruisers from the sheriff's office drove full speed up the dirt road. Dust trailed as it kicked up from behind the cars. The blue lights flashed.

Alex waited for them as she stepped out of her Jeep and handed them the envelope with the pictures Allen had taken the night of Bonnie's death.

Amanda stood up from the picnic table and looked toward the officers coming toward us. She turned and stepped toward the live oak behind her.

I was sure she was going to take off. I said, "Amanda, don't. You can't run."

"I know," she said as she reached around the base of the tree. She grabbed a thick rope that was loosely tied around the trunk, and with both hands she pulled herself up to a thick limb less than ten feet over her head.

Like a monkey, she climbed up and sat on the limb, her feet hanging down.

"What the hell are you doing?" I said. "You have to come down."

Two officers stood next to me as we all looked up at her. One of them said, "Ma'am, please come down from that tree."

"I will," she said. She threw the rope around her neck and pulled the loop tight.

I looked back at Alex as she stood at her Jeep with one of the other officers.

"*Amanda!*" I yelled as I watched her up in the tree. "What are you doing?" I turned, looked at the officers standing behind me with their hands on their holsters. "*Do something!*"

The same officer again looked up at her. "Come down here right now, ma'am."

"Amanda," I said, "Please... whatever you're doing. Stop right now. Don't do this."

I turned and looked at Alex and as soon as she looked our way she ran toward us, under the tree.

Alex yelled, "*Amanda, stop!*"

We both looked up at Amanda.

With the rope around her neck, Amanda climbed up onto another limb, far out of anyone's reach. She was a long way from the ground. And before I could say another word, she jumped.

It happened as if it was in slow motion.

I wasn't sure if I froze or was unable to move, but I felt helpless.

Amanda kicked her feet as they hung just over my head.

Alex screamed and pushed me aside, "*Get out of the way!*" She pulled her Glock from her holster and pointed it up and over Amanda's head.

Amanda choked as she had her fingers between the rope and the skin of her neck.

I tried to jump for her but Alex yelled again, "*Get down!*"

"Alex what the hell are you—"

I ducked as Alex fired a shot from her gun, up toward the limb.

Amanda dropped from the tree. The long rope fell on top of her as she hit the ground with the loop still tied around her neck. She rolled over, coughing and choking as she struggled to get the rope loose.

One of the officers crouched down to help her.

I looked up at what was left of the rope, still tied around the limb. I glanced back at Alex as she tucked her Glock into her holster. "Nice shot," I said.

The other officers on the ground next to Amanda looked up at Alex and nodded in agreement.

"I was afraid I'd hit one of you."

I looked toward the garage and saw Luis.

He stood outside the building then ran toward us. "*Amanda!*"

The officers drew their weapons. One of them yelled toward Luis. "*Stop right there!*"

But Luis kept running toward us. "Amanda, what are you doing?"

The officer kept his weapon pointed at Luis. "*Stop!* Don't take one more step."

Luis listened. He raised his hands over his head and stopped twenty yards from where we were standing. "Is she okay?" he said with his eyes on Amanda.

Alex nodded, "She's okay."

Amanda looked up at Luis, "Don't do anything stupid. They know everything."

Luis looked around at me and Alex and the officers. "*Everything?*"

Chapter 36

THE ST. JOHNS RIVER was a little rough with the storm that'd passed. The water slapped up against the side of my boat. But the sky was calm and blue with a tint of orange as the sun started to set.

Another resident from Trout River Marina walked toward me as I sat out on the dock. He had a woman I'd never seen before under his arm and gave me a nod. "Henry, we're heading for the bar, if you want to join us?"

I raised my glass as he walked past. "I think I'll just sit out here, take in everything I've missed the past few months."

He turned to me over his shoulder. "Good to have you back, Henry."

Alex pulled her Jeep into a space in the parking lot. I watched her as she stepped out and walked toward me with what looked like a six pack in her hand.

I got up, pulled another chair out from my boat and opened it up next to me on the dock. I finished what was left in my glass and poured another Jack Daniels just as she approached.

"Just hung up with Mike. Luis is in custody."

"Did he confess?"

She shook her head. "They found the gun at his cousin's shop. Had Luis's fingerprints all over it."

I took a sip from my glass. "I still say he did it to protect Amanda. He knew Allen had something that'd help prove what happened."

Alex shrugged. "Can I see what they gave you?"

"Who?"

"The doctor."

"You don't believe me?"

Alex cracked open one of her beers and took a sip. "No, not really."

"They said my reaction to the concussion was worse, since it wasn't my first."

"How many have you had?" she said.

I shrugged. "I don't know. Five?"

"Are you serious?"

"The doctor told me to do whatever I can to relax. Try yoga or something." I held up my glass. "She didn't mention having a few drinks, but I'm sure it helps."

"So you're going to live?"

I laughed. "She recommended more than three hours of sleep each night."

Alex rolled her eyes. "You needed a doctor to tell you that?" She put her beer down on the dock and stood up from her chair.

I turned and looked up at her as she walked behind me. "What are you doing?"

She started to rub my shoulders.

I closed my eyes and—as the doctor ordered—tried to relax.

But it was easier said than done.

"You know, I was thinking earlier. How can we be so sure Amanda didn't kill Allen?"

Alex stopped what she was doing. "Well, they're still investigating. But, the truth is, I think at this point you have to let it go. Let the sheriff's office do their job. You did what you were paid to do."

I turned and looked up at her. "To be honest, I don't think James would've hired me if he knew his sister was the one who killed Bonnie."

"Probably not." She continued to rub my shoulders.

I finally started to relax. "You don't have to do that," I said. But I didn't want her to stop. I closed my eyes for what seemed like a moment.

· · · · ● · ● · · ·

It was dark when I opened my eyes, although the street lamps around the marina kept things fairly bright.

Alex was still seated next to me, although it looked like her six pack was down to three.

I wiped the corner of my mouth with the back of my hand. "Jesus, how long was I out?"

Alex shrugged. "Twenty minutes."

I stood up from the chair and stretched my arms above my head. "I'm wiped out."

"I wonder why," she said. "You don't stop, Henry. I realize you were working a case, but you're going to kill yourself if you keep at it the way you do."

I reached down and poured a shot into my glass. "You're not going to give me another speech about my drinking, are you?"

Alex waited a moment before she answered. "I guess not."

A white BMW pulled into the lot and drove toward us, the brights beams in our eyes.

I put my arm up to block the headlights as James walked toward us.

Normally a client would be a little more relieved to have the answer they were hoping for. But not in this case, as was expected.

I stood from the chair and stepped toward him. "How's she doing?"

James shrugged. "Okay, I guess. She's at my house... got a monitor on her ankle. She can't go anywhere until the trial. As long as we can prove it was really an accident..."

"I do believe her," I said.

"Did the attorney call you yet?" James said.

"Her attorney?" I shook my head. "No, not yet. Why?"

He looked past me, toward my boat. His face got a bit twisted. "You really live here now, instead of that beautiful space near the beach?"

I turned back, glanced at the boat. "It needs some work, but it's home."

"You gave up a prime location..." James said.

"Depends what you want," I said. I reached down for my glass and took a sip. "Can I get you a drink?"

James shook his head and handed me the envelope he'd been holding in his hands. "I'm going to need to hire you again, to help the attorney. I'll pay you up front."

I waved him off. "I'll give you everything I have. Photos... witness accounts. But, I don't think there's anything else I can add."

James looked out toward the St. Johns for a moment. With his back to me, he said, "Amanda's all I've got left." He turned to me as he wiped his hand against his cheek, just under his eye. "She can't go to prison..."

Alex reached for the envelope. "We'll do what we can to help." She smiled as James and I both gave her a look.

"I believe her," Alex said. "And Henry does too. So we'll do whatever we can to help you and her get through this."

James looked back and forth from me to Alex. "I appreciate it." He turned and walked away toward his car.

I waited for him to step into his car and turned to Alex. "I don't know if there's enough to prove she's innocent."

Alex looked toward the parking lot as James drove away. She opened the envelope, looked inside, and pulled out the check made out to *Walsh Investigations*. She folded it in half and stuck it in her pocket. "James is depending on us. So is Amanda. All we can do is do our best."

I looked up at her and smiled. "If you want to change the name... Walsh-Jepson Investigations has a nice ring to it."

Alex shook her head as she stepped behind me and again began to rub my shoulders.

I reached up for her hand.

She said, "As long as we're splitting the checks, I don't care what you put on the sign."

• • • • • • • • • •

Thank you for reading *The Night the Music Died*. The mysteries continue with the fifth book in the Henry Walsh Private Investigator series, *Dead Men Don't Smile*. Find out more and grab the latest book at GregoryPayette.com

Sign up for the newsletter on my website:

GregoryPayette.com

Once or twice a month I'll send you updates and news. Plus, you'll be the first to hear about new releases with special prices. If you'd like to receive the Henry Walsh prequel (for free) use the sign-up form here: **GregoryPayette.com/crossroad**

Also by Gregory Payette

Visit GregoryPayette.com for the complete catalog:

HENRY WALSH MYSTERIES

Dead at Third

The Last Ride

The Crystal Pelican

The Night the Music Died

Dead Men Don't Smile

Dead in the Creek

Dropped Dead

Dead Luck

A Shot in the Dark

JOE SHELDON SERIES

Play It Cool

Play It Again

Play It Down

U.S. MARSHAL CHARLIE HARLOW

Shake the Trees

Trackdown

JAKE HORN MYSTERIES

Murder at Morrissey Motel

STANDALONES

Biscayne Boogie

Tell Them I'm Dead

Drag the Man Down

Half Cocked

Danny Womack's .38

Printed in the USA
CPSIA information can be obtained
at www.ICGtesting.com
CBHW030536020524
7906CB00002B/52